SOMNOLENCIA

THE NAP THAT
CONQUERED THE WORLD

GUFRAN KHAN

INDIA • SINGAPORE • MALAYSIA

ISBN

Hardcase 979-8-89777-658-0
Paperback 979-8-89724-592-5

Disclaimer

Somnolencia: The Nap That Conquered the World is a work of fiction. Any resemblance to real-life workaholics, corporate overlords, or self-proclaimed "grindset" enthusiasts is purely coincidental (or, perhaps, eerily accurate). This novel is a satirical exploration of the modern world's obsession with productivity, its disregard for rest, and the eternal struggle between relaxation and relentless ambition. If this book makes you reconsider your caffeine intake or question, why you're always tired - good. You probably need a nap.

Dedication

To my beloved parents, Zameer Khan and Haseena Begum, whose unconditional love and sacrifices have shaped the person I am today.

To my wonderful wife, Umme Amra, whose unwavering support and encouragement have been my greatest strength.

To my precious children, Mohammad Zayaan Khan and Mohammad Shayaan Khan, who fill my days with joy and remind me of the magic of dreams and storytelling.

To my father-in-law and mentor, Khalid Ahmed, whose wisdom has guided me through life's challenges.

To my first manager, Syed Taher, who played a pivotal role in my early journey, and to my mentor, Vikram Verma, whose leadership and vision continue to inspire me.

To my brothers, sisters, brothers-in-law, and sisters-in-law, whose love and support have been a constant source of motivation.

To my friends and colleagues, who stood by me through this journey, believing in me even when I doubted myself.

This novel would not have been possible without each of you. It belongs as much to you as it does to me. Thank you for being part of my story.

Synopsis

In the land of Somnolencia, where naps are sacred and rest is revered, an ancient enemy rises the ideology of Productivity Without Pause. Sir Industrious, the tireless visionary, and Sir Never-Stops, the relentless machine of efficiency, wage war against leisure, seeking to transform the world into an empire of endless Labour.

But in a world where sleep is strength, a resistance forms. Led by the legendary Council of Naps, the people of Somnolencia must fight back, armed with The Eternal Snooze Button, the wisdom of The Dozing Sage, and the revolutionary belief that doing nothing is, in fact, everything.

As the battle between workaholism and restfulness escalates, the fate of The Great Nap hangs in the balance. Can Somnolencia reclaim its right to sleep, or will the world awaken to an era where rest is outlawed?

A whimsical, satirical, and thought-provoking journey into the absurdities of modern life, Somnolencia: The Nap That Conquered the World is an ode to the power of sleep and a warning against the cult of busyness.

Table of Contents

Prologue: The World That Forgot to Rest

Long ago, before the rise of the Sleepless Ones, the world was at peace. Fields of plush pillows stretched across the land, rivers of chamomile tea flowed endlessly, and the sacred Pillow Prophecies foretold of a future where rest was eternal.

But not all were content. In the shadows, a movement stirred - whispers of efficiency, echoes of tireless ambition. Sir Industrious, the dreamer of endless toil, saw the world not as a haven, but as an opportunity. He saw untapped hours, wasted potential, and the curse of stillness.

And so, the Age of Restlessness began.

One by one, the kingdoms of leisure fell. The Festival of Idleness was outlawed, the Napfluencers were silenced, and the sacred Siesta Shrines were dismantled. The world grew brighter, noisier, faster. People traded dreams for deadlines, yawns for coffee, and peace for productivity.

But even in the darkest night, embers of defiance remained.

Now, as the Great Awakening Storm gathers, the final battle looms. The champions of sleep must rise, for if they fail…

The world will never rest again.

A World Asleep, A World Awake

In the world we live in, alarms scream us into consciousness, productivity trackers measure our worth, and exhaustion is worn like a badge of honour. We race against deadlines, battle burnout, and chase an ever-moving finish line called "success." The modern world glorifies hustle culture, where sleep is sacrificed on the altar of efficiency, and rest is seen as weakness.

Every day, millions wake up to the blaring demands of a world that never slows down. Coffee cups stack like battle trophies, emails pile up before sunrise, and the mere thought of slowing down invites guilt. Do more. Be more. Work harder. Sleep later. These are the mantras of the age, whispered in offices, classrooms, and factory floors alike.

But what if everything we've been told about work and success is wrong? What if the true secret to power, wisdom, and happiness wasn't endless toil - but rest?

A World on the Edge of Awakening

Welcome to Somnolencia, a land where naps are sacred, hustle is heresy, and dreaming is the highest form of rebellion.

Here, drowsy philosophers debate the meaning of leisure, legendary nappers hold wisdom greater than kings, and the ultimate battle isn't between good and evil but between rest and relentless labour.

For centuries, Somnolencia thrived in peaceful slumber, ruled by the wisdom of The Great Nap Council and guided by the ancient texts of The Pillow Prophecies. The people lived in harmony with the rhythms of rest, undisturbed by the madness of productivity.

But something is changing.

A disturbance ripples through the fabric of dreams. A dark force is stirring, threatening to rattle Somnolencia from its blissful haze. The shadows lengthen as whispers spread of an ancient and terrible curse; a force so powerful it could break the cycle of sleep itself.

They call it The Curse of the Spring Forward - a dreaded prophecy of an unnatural event where an hour is stolen from time itself, disrupting sleep, breaking dreams, and shaking the foundation of rest.

At the heart of this chaos stands Zzzocrates, the revered sage of slumber, staring into the abyss of time with weary eyes. He knows what is coming. He knows that once the first hour is lost, others will follow. That one stolen hour will lead to a war against rest itself.

And so, the struggle begins.

As the bells of Somnolencia tremble and the land stirs in unease, the battle lines are drawn - not between good and evil, but between those who wish to sleep and those who would tear it away.

The Curse of the Spring Forward is upon them.

And if Somnolencia falls, will the real world be next?

The Curse of the Spring Forward

It was the most dreaded time of the year in Somnolencia. A moment so feared, so loathed, that even the most resilient nappers whispered its name with trembling lips.

The Spring Forward.

Each year, when the cursed moment arrived, an entire hour vanished into the void—stolen, erased, never to be seen again. One moment, the people of Somnolencia were curled up in blissful slumber, and the next, their clocks betrayed them.

One hour. Gone. As if some invisible thief had plucked it from the fabric of time itself.

The Council of Naps Convenes

The Council of Naps gathered in emergency session, their silken robes of leisure barely concealing their barely awake panic. The great hall of the Temple of Tranquillity was packed with drowsy citizens, each clutching their weighted blankets and warm mugs of chamomile tea, their faces twisted in outrage.

"This is an act of war!" cried Madame Siesta LaFleur, clutching her pearl-embroidered sleep mask. "An hour of sleep has been taken from us without consent! Without due process!"

"The injustice!" moaned Grand Poobah Lethargio, sprawled dramatically across a pile of silk cushions. "This is unnatural! Evil! I demand reparations in the form of a weeklong nap!"

"Let us not panic," murmured Zzzocrates, stroking his beard thoughtfully. "Let us first investigate who is responsible for this heinous crime."

The answer, of course, was clear.

The Chronomancers of the Waking World.

These sinister time-warping bureaucrats, obsessed with schedules and efficiency, had once again imposed their cruel decree upon the land: Daylight Savings Time.

A spell so powerful, so absurdly arbitrary, that it sent even the most seasoned sleepers into a spiral of confusion and existential dread.

Even worse, its effects were immediate.

The Symptoms of the Spring Forward Curse:

The Great Morning Stumble – Citizens awoke in a daze, wandering the streets like sleep-deprived zombies, unsure of what year it was.

The Yawn plague – A chain reaction of unstoppable yawns spread through the land, incapacitating entire districts.

The Unbearable Lightness of Being Awake Too Soon – The sun, that wretched overachiever, had risen earlier, mocking them all with its punctuality.

The Prophecy of the Snooze Sages

Deep within the Temple of Tranquillity, the Snooze Sages-the oldest and wisest of Somnolencia's dreamers had foreseen this catastrophe. The Pillow Prophecies, ancient texts woven into the softest memory-foam scrolls, spoke of a time when sleep itself would be threatened by the relentless advance of productivity.

"The time-thieves shall come," intoned Master Yawnrick, the eldest of the sages, his voice slow and deliberate. "They will steal our hours and force us to rise before we are ready. Only through the power of the Eternal Snooze shall we restore the balance."

A murmur spread through the council. The Eternal Snooze Button - a legendary artifact said to grant unbreakable, infinite rest—was thought to be mere myth. But if it truly existed, it could undo the effects of the Spring Forward once and for all.

The Quest for the Eternal Snooze

And so, it was decided: a group of Somnolencia's bravest (and least energetic) warriors would embark on a great journey to retrieve the Eternal Snooze Button before it was too late.

The Fellowship of the Nap was formed:

Sir Drowsius the Ever-Dreaming, wielder of the Weighted Blanket of Comfort.

Napoleon Dozebart, a brilliant strategist known for his power naps in the heat of battle.

Countess Slumberly, who could lull even the most restless soul into peaceful sleep with her lullabies.

Their mission: to venture into the dreaded Perpetual Wakefulness, the domain of the Chronomancers, and reclaim the lost hour.

The Battle of the Snooze

Their journey led them to The Tower of Unrelenting Alarms, where the Chronomancers hoarded stolen minutes like a dragon hoards gold. As the Fellowship approached, the air was thick with the sound of ticking clocks and the distant ringing of morning alarms - an oppressive, nightmarish cacophony designed to keep even the most stubborn sleeper awake.

The battle was unlike anything Somnolencia had ever seen. Nap Grenades (pouches of lavender and chamomile) were lobbed into the tower, putting several lesser Chronomancers into a dazed stupor. Napoleon Dozebart led the charge, his Pillow Shield absorbing a direct blast from the Horn of Urgency - a terrible weapon that could induce panic over imaginary deadlines.

But just as the Eternal Snooze Button was within their grasp, The Lord of the Timetable - the head Chronomancers himself - appeared.

"You fools," he sneered, adjusting his meticulously scheduled planner. "You think you can stop time? You think you can win against the march of progress?"

He lifted his Hourglass Staff, preparing to accelerate time even further.

Then, from the shadows, a new figure emerged.

A woman dressed in sleek, metallic robes, her arms filled with ledgers, schedules, and an overwhelming number of unfinished tasks.

Lady Multitaska.

The Council of Naps gasped. A name spoken only in fear.

"You lazy dreamers," she scoffed. "Sleep is a crutch for the inefficient. Only through endless motion can true productivity be achieved."

The Fellowship barely had time to react before she unleashed her most devastating attack:

The Cascade of Infinite Deadlines.

Suddenly, lists of unfinished tasks flooded the battlefield, drowning the warriors in an overwhelming sense of obligations. Napoleon Dozebart tried to swipe them away with his Pillow Shield, but the weight of uncompleted reports, unanswered messages, and overdue projects was too great.

Sir Drowsius collapsed under the stress, mumbling something about "just five more minutes."

Countess Slumberly tried to sing a lullaby, but even her voice was drowned out by the insidious whispers of pending responsibilities.

The Fellowship was losing.

And in the distance, Somnolencia itself began to stir restlessly.

If something was not done soon, the city—their home—would awaken.

As the dust settled, and the Fellowship of the Nap barely managed to escape with their dreams intact, one thing was clear: this was no longer just a battle for an hour of sleep.

This was a war for the soul of Somnolencia.

If the forces of wakefulness continued their advance, if Lady Multitaska and the Chronomancers were not stopped, the very concept of rest could be erased forever.

And so, deep within the hidden dream-temples, a new movement began to stir.

A rebellion.

The Nocturnal Rebellion.

For the Wide-Awake Few, those who had been cursed with restlessness, had finally had enough.

The time had come to fight back.

And this time, they would not wake until they had won.

03

The Nocturnal Rebellion

The city of Somnolencia had always been a sanctuary of sleep, a haven where naps were sacred, and rest was an unassailable right. But now, an unsettling phenomenon had begun to spread through its drowsy streets. Some citizens, once devoted to the art of relaxation, could no longer find peace in their slumber.

They were The Wide-Awake Few.

Their plight was a cruel irony. Sleep was all they had ever known, and now, it was being taken from them.

The Curse of the Restless

It started with whispers in the night. At first, only a handful of dreamers found themselves tossing and turning, unable to drift into their usual blissful slumber. Then, the affliction spread. Whole households sat in their moonlit homes, eyes wide, staring into the darkness.

The Council of Naps convened an emergency meeting at The Hall of Eternal Yawns. Zzzocrates, his eyelids drooping with concern, addressed the chamber:

"This," he murmured, rubbing his temple, "is most unnatural. Never before have our people suffered from a night without dreams."

Madame Siesta LaFleur, normally draped in elegance and calm, looked deeply troubled. "Something is amiss," she declared. "Our people do not choose wakefulness. It has been forced upon them."

Even the ever-composed Grand Poobah Lethargio let out a sigh heavier than usual. "We must uncover the cause," he decreed, stretching luxuriously in his reclining chair. "But first, a moment of contemplation."

That "moment" turned into a three-hour collective nap, but the problem remained when they awoke.

The Rise of the Sleepless Insurgents

Among the afflicted was a former nap enthusiast known as Captain Tosswell. He had once been an elite member of the Dream Brigade, tasked with enforcing the sacred Midday Nap Mandate. But now, deprived of rest, he had become a shadow of his former self.

"We must fight back!" Tosswell declared to a group of fellow insomniacs. "If sleep no longer welcomes us, then we must forge a new path!"

And so, The Nocturnal Rebellion was born.

By the light of the Two-Yawned Moon, they gathered in dark alleys, their eyes bloodshot, their movements jittery.

They raided pillow warehouses, seeking comfort. They occupied The Temple of Tranquility, demanding answers. Their leader, Lady Wakefield, preached a radical doctrine:

"If we cannot sleep, then we must embrace the wakefulness!"

This was heresy. To defy the cycle of sleep and waking was to defy the very essence of Somnolencia.

The Council of Naps dispatched envoys to reason with them, offering warm milk, soothing lullabies, even the sacred Weighted Blankets of the Ancients. But it was no use. The Wide-Awake Few were too far gone.

"We will not rest!" they shouted, their voices shaking. "Not until we uncover the truth!"

A Perilous Discovery

And uncover it they did. Deep beneath the city, in the abandoned chambers of the Yawning Catacombs, they found an ancient device - one that hummed with an unnatural energy.

Zzzocrates and Madame Siesta LaFleur arrived, summoned by an urgent distress signal. What they saw made their hearts sink.

The device pulsed with an eerie, neon glow. Its tubes bubbled with a liquid that smelled sharp and unnatural - a scent unlike anything Somnolencia had ever known.

"This… this is not of our world," Madame Siesta whispered.

Tosswell turned to them, his voice hollow. "We've been poisoned. Our sleeplessness… it is not a curse of the mind. It was done to us."

The realization sent a shudder through the room.

Zzzocrates narrowed his eyes, rubbing his forehead as if already exhausted by the implications. "Then the question is not why we cannot sleep."

His gaze darkened.

"It is who wants us awake and for what purpose."

The Dawn of a Dark Conspiracy

As they debated, a slow, rhythmic drip echoed through the chamber. A single drop of the glowing liquid oozed from a cracked pipe, landing on the stone floor.

Captain Tosswell bent down and touched the substance. Instantly, he jolted upright. His pupils dilated. His fingers twitched.

A manic grin spread across his face.

"I… I feel alive."

And that was when they realized the true horror.

This was not just a sleep disorder. It was a deliberate act of sabotage. Someone somewhere had introduced a stimulant into the city's lifeblood.

Something that stole rest.

Something that forced wakefulness.

And it was spreading.

A New Threat Awakens: The Energy Drink Epidemic

Zzzocrates turned to Madame Siesta LaFleur. "If this… concoction reaches the masses"

Madame Siesta's face paled. "Then sleep will no longer be a choice."

Grand Poobah Lethargio's voice was grave. "Then we are no longer facing a rebellion of the few."

He turned to the rising dawn, where the first perky, jittering figures were emerging from the shadows of the city.

"We are facing an epidemic."

And so, the true battle began.

The Battle for Sleep had been a fight for tradition.

The War of Stillness had been a fight for survival.

But now, Somnolencia would face its greatest trial yet.

The Energy Drink Epidemic was coming.

And if they could not stop it, Somnolencia itself might never sleep again.

04

The Energy Drink Epidemic

It started subtly. A few citizens of Somnolencia reported feeling a strange tingling in their fingers. Then, twitching. Then, an unfamiliar urge to move.

At first, the Council of Naps dismissed these complaints as anomalies. Perhaps these individuals had simply napped too lightly the night before, or worse, attempted a short nap that never reached the sacred REM cycle. But then, the symptoms spread.

The city's famed Yawn Gardens, normally filled with content citizens dozing beneath the shade of colossal Slumberberry trees, now played host to a terrifying sight—people pacing in circles, unable to sit still.

The public hammocks, once overflowing with Somnolencians wrapped in blissful repose, were abandoned.

Worst of all, the Temple of Tranquility, where monks practiced the ancient art of the Eternal Afternoon Nap, was in utter chaos. Some monks had begun chanting at twice the normal speed, their mantras slurring into a nervous babble. Others were seen jogging in place, their eyes wide, their sacred robes drenched in sweat.

And then, the first true horror struck.

Sir Snoremore, the legendary elder of the Order of Perpetual Drowsiness - a man who had held the world record for the longest continuous nap - opened his eyes.

And he could not close them again.

The Dark Origins of the Concoction

Zzzocrates and Madame Siesta LaFleur hurried to the Yawning Catacombs, where Captain Tosswell and his Nocturnal Rebels had discovered the unholy substance - the one that had stolen their sleep.

A single drop had transformed Tosswell into a jittery, hyper-aware insomniac, and now, they knew for certain:

This was no accident.

"This foul potion has spread beyond our walls," Madame Siesta said, examining the glowing residue still clinging to the catacomb's machinery. "But who could have done this?"

A shadow stirred in the dim corridor. A spy - one of Tosswell's scouts - rushed into the chamber, panting.

"My lords… we have seen it! It has a name!"

Zzzocrates raised a weary brow. "What is it called?"

The scout hesitated, as if speaking the name alone might shatter the peace of Somnolencia forever.

Then, in a hushed, almost reverent whisper, he said:

"Energy drinks."

The Rise of the Perpetually Perky

The conspiracy came crashing down all at once.

Through the hidden network of Underground Sleepwalkers, the Council of Naps uncovered the source of the corruption.

An ancient facility, long forgotten beneath the cobbled streets of Somnolencia, had been reactivated. And there, hidden in the darkness, great machines churned out glowing vats of the unholy liquid.

Bottles of Vigoraid, HyperBoost, and the most fearsome of them all - EndlessGo™ - were being distributed across the land.

The more the citizens drank, the less they slept.

The less they slept, the more they worked.

And the more they worked, the more productive they became.

A horrifying new order was rising, one that threatened to undo everything Somnolencia had ever stood for.

At the heart of this caffeinated conspiracy stood a new and fearsome enemy - Lady Multitaska, the Grand Administrator of Perpetuopolis.

Once a mere assistant to Sir Industrious the Tireless, Lady Multitaska had seized power after his fall, determined to complete his vision. Where Industrious sought to conquer Somnolencia through force, she sought to do it through stimulation.

"The people do not need rest," she declared from her glowing caffeine throne deep within the Perkulatorium, the headquarters of the Hyper-Efficiency Bureau. "They need energy. They need focus. And most of all" - her sharp eyes glittered - "they need to keep moving."

With each passing hour, her Energy Drink Empire expanded.

The people of Somnolencia, once known for their ability to sleep anywhere, at any time, were forgetting how.

And in their place rose a new breed of citizen - the Perpetually Perky.

Desperate to counteract the epidemic, the Council of Naps devised a bold plan.

If they could not convince the people to rest, they would force them.

Zzzocrates, Madame Siesta, and Captain Tosswell gathered the last remaining Sleepwalkers and devised a mission unlike any before.

"We must reclaim the symbol of our people," Zzzocrates declared, his voice steady. "The one thing that can bring them back from the brink."

Madame Siesta nodded. "The Great Mattress of Somnolencia."

The legendary artifact, woven from the Threads of Dreaming, had the power to restore even the most restless soul. But there was only one problem.

Lady Multitaska had stolen it.

And so, The Great Mattress Heist was born - the most ambitious, most absurd, and most gloriously drowsy crime ever attempted.

Would they succeed? Could the people of Somnolencia be saved? Or was this, the final waking hour?

Only time would tell.

05

The Great Mattress Heist

Beneath the dim glow of the Yawning Lanterns, the Council of Naps gathered in the secret underground chamber of the Pillow Prophets. The situation in Somnolencia had deteriorated rapidly. The Perpetually Perky, driven by energy drinks, overclocked schedules, and relentless motion, were now completely under Lady Multitaska's grip.

Their beloved Great Mattress of Somnolencia, a relic said to possess the power to restore even the most unrested soul, had been taken to Perpetuopolis - the sprawling, sleepless capital of Lady Multitaska's regime. Without it, the people of Somnolencia had no hope of recovering from the energy drink epidemic.

The only solution?

Steal it back.

"This is no ordinary theft," Zzzocrates warned, rolling out an ancient scroll onto the Velvet Table of Tranquility. The map displayed a fortress of ceaseless activity, where lights never dimmed, clocks never stopped, and to-do lists grew faster than they could be completed.

Lady Multitaska had hidden the Great Mattress within the Vault of Maximum Efficiency, deep within the Perkulatorium - a place no drowsy being had ever dared step foot in.

Captain Tosswell, leader of the Nocturnal Rebellion, clenched his fists. "That mattress belongs to the people of Somnolencia. If we don't get it back, we're doomed to endless wakefulness."

Madame Siesta LaFleur nodded solemnly. "We must infiltrate Perpetuopolis, bypass the Bureau of Hyper-Efficiency, and retrieve the mattress before they know what's happening."

Zzzocrates sighed, rubbing his temples. "We have but one chance. And we'll need the finest talents Somnolencia has to offer"

The Dream Team

To pull off this heist of the century, they gathered a team of specialists:

Madame Siesta LaFleur – Master of Sleep-Fu and expert in dream-state infiltration.

Captain Tosswell – Former victim of the energy drink plague, now the leader of the resistance.

Sir Snoremore – The once-perpetual napper, still struggling to regain his legendary sleep, but armed with hypnotic snoring techniques.

Dozer, the Silent – A legendary thief known for sneaking past alarm clocks, phone notifications, and even the dreaded early morning meetings.

Professor Slumberson – Theoretical nap physicist, tasked with calculating the precise moment of drowsiness needed for infiltration.

The Duvet Duo – Two identical twins who could roll anyone into a burrito of blankets in mere seconds.

Armed with nothing but pillows, blankets, and an absurdly well-thought-out plan, the team set off toward Perpetuopolis, where Lady Multitaska's forces waited.

The Infiltration of the Perkulatorium

The journey was perilous. They had to sneak past:

The Treadmill Brigades, whose soldiers never stopped running.

The Alarm Bell Towers, which rang every five minutes to prevent napping.

The Hyper-Focus Snipers, trained to detect signs of sluggishness.

Disguised as productivity consultants, the team bluffed their way inside, pretending to promote the newest efficiency methods (which, ironically, involved short power naps).

Once inside the Perkulatorium, they navigated through mazes of filing cabinets, endless spreadsheets, and never-ending brainstorming meetings until they reached, The Vault of Maximum Efficiency.

There it was. The Great Mattress of Somnolencia, floating atop a platform of eternal wakefulness.

But just as they reached for it, alarms blared.

Lady Multitaska's Counterattack

"You actually thought you could steal from me?"

The voice rang from above, cutting through the air like the sharp snap of a productivity planner shutting closed.

Lady Multitaska stood upon a tower of task lists, clad in a robe woven from overlapping calendars.

"Somnolencia is finished," she declared, stepping forward. "Your people have already adapted to the new world order - one of constant wakefulness, endless meetings, and boundless multitasking."

"You've gone too far, Multitaska!" Captain Tosswell shouted. "Sleep is essential! Naps are a sacred right!"

Lady Multitaska scoffed. "Oh, really? Then why do my people get so much done?"

With a snap of her fingers, her Hyper-Workers emerged - former Somnolencians now fully converted to Perpetuopolitan discipline. Their eyes twitched with caffeinated fervour. Their hands juggled multiple projects simultaneously. They answered emails before they were even sent.

The heist had become a battle for Somnolencia's very soul.

The Great Escape & The Cost of Victory

The Dream Team fought bravely.

Dozer the Silent snuck past the Hyper-Workers, untying the Mattress's restraints.

Sir Snoremore unleashed a Hypno-Snore, causing the enemy to momentarily pause and yawn.

Madame Siesta used her signature move, the Duvet Dropkick - to entangle Lady Multitaska in a weighted blanket.

With one final push, they secured the mattress, rolled it onto a Sleepwagon, and fled into the night.

But as they escaped Perpetuopolis, the sky shifted.

Something was wrong.

Lady Multitaska, though bound in blankets, laughed.

"You think you've won," she called out, "but the damage has already been done!"

And as she spoke, the clock towers of Perpetuopolis rang in unison.

Zzzocrates paled. He turned to Professor Slumberson, who clutched his ancient timepiece.

"This… this isn't just a normal hour," the professor whispered in horror. "She's activated The Spring Forward."

"No," Captain Tosswell gasped. "Not the Daylight Savings Curse."

Lady Multitaska smirked. "Enjoy your precious mattress, fools. But when the sun rises, an hour will be stolen from time itself. And not even the deepest nap will bring it back."

The Dream Team had won the Great Mattress Heist.

But at what terrible cost?

As the first light of dawn crept over the horizon, the hour vanished.

And with it, the balance of sleep and wakefulness was about to be shattered.

06

The Tragedy of the Stolen Hour

The sun rose too soon over Somnolencia.

It was a morning unlike any other - one that felt wrong, as though the night had been snatched away before it could fully embrace its weary dreamers. The people of Somnolencia awoke disoriented, sluggish, and deeply confused.

"What happened?" a groggy voice muttered in the town square.

"I swear it was 3 AM just moments ago," another yawned, staring at the sundial, which seemed to be mocking them.

Zzzocrates stumbled out of his library, his silken nightcap askew. "It's happened," he croaked. "The hour... it's been stolen."

Captain Tosswell, still sore from the Great Mattress Heist, turned to Professor Slumberson. "Tell me it's reversible."

The professor shook his head grimly. "It never is. This is the Curse of the Spring Forward - an ancient time trickery designed to rob the world of an hour of sleep every year."

The people gasped. Some clutched their pillows in horror.

But Lady Multitaska's sinister plan was far from over.

The Mechanics of the Time Theft

Zzzocrates unfurled an ancient scroll from The Pillow Prophecies, detailing the mechanics of this foul sorcery.

"The Spring Forward was first devised by the Cult of Productivity, a shadowy sect that believed sleep was a hindrance to efficiency. Long ago, they bargained with the Chronomancers, demanding that an hour be stripped from time itself in the name of progress."

He gestured toward the Tower of the Chronomancers, an ancient structure at the heart of Perpetuopolis. "They control time from there. Every year, on this cursed day, they shift the clocks forward stealing an hour from the world."

Captain Tosswell clenched his fists. "So we can get it back?"

"No," Professor Slumberson said. "It doesn't work that way. The hour is not simply taken - it is unmade."

A heavy silence fell over Somnolencia.

Zzzocrates sighed. "This is why people wander around on this day feeling lost, exhausted, and irritable. The stolen hour exists in a limbo between wakefulness and dreams. And worst of all, this is only the beginning."

The Sleepologists nodded grimly. "First, we lose an hour," one of them muttered, "then, the sleeplessness spreads."

The Unfolding Catastrophe

Somnolencia quickly descended into chaos.

The usually blissful town square turned into a festival of exhaustion:

Nap schedules were thrown into disarray. People woke up either too early or too late, confused about how time even worked anymore.

The Snore Choir - renowned for their synchronized afternoon dozes, collapsed into a cacophony of mismatched yawns.

The Grand Nappers of Somnolencia, the revered elders who could sleep through anything, now tossed and turned in frustration, muttering about how things had been better "back in the good old days of endless sleep."

Sleep-deprived Somnolencians tried to function, but their legs dragged, their eyelids fluttered, and their thoughts dissolved into half-dreams of warm blankets and soft pillows.

The worst part?

The Perpetually Perky were unaffected.

Lady Multitaska's hyper-efficient followers, fuelled by an unnatural wakefulness, stormed into Somnolencia with smug expressions and pre-filled spreadsheets.

"Oh no," Madame Siesta groaned. "It's starting."

"Starting?" Captain Tosswell asked.

Zzzocrates narrowed his eyes. "The Cult of Productivity will come next."

As if summoned by their very words, a group of suited figures marched into the town square. Their leader, a tall, imposing figure in a pinstriped robe of uninterrupted wakefulness, stepped forward.

"I am Overseer Hustlebane," he declared, his voice smooth yet relentlessly driven. "And we have come to offer you a better way."

The townsfolk of Somnolencia, still reeling from the stolen hour, barely had the strength to question him.

"We know you feel tired," Hustlebane continued, spreading his arms in a practiced gesture of persuasion. "That's because you are stuck in the old ways. But fear not, there is a solution."

The Cultists stepped forward, offering productivity guides, planners, and cursed magical stones known as 'Task Trackers.'

"Through constant motion, through efficiency, through the complete eradication of naps, you too can ascend to a higher plane of function."

A hush fell over the crowd.

Then, one voice spoke up.

"No."

All eyes turned to Zzzocrates.

"You may have stolen our hour," he said, stepping forward, his robes of slumber billowing in the morning wind, "but you will not steal our dreams."

Hustlebane smirked. "Dreams? My dear philosopher, dreams are dead weight. They hold you back. We have progress to make, a world to optimize."

The Cultists cheered.

But Zzzocrates did not waver.

"You do not understand," he said, raising his voice. "We are not merely tired people. We are guardians of the nap. We are defenders of the doze. You think motion is the answer? No, dear Hustlebane. We know the truth."

Hustlebane narrowed his eyes. "And what truth is that?"

Zzzocrates smiled.

"The Myth of Productivity."

Hustlebane's smirk faltered.

And with that, Zzzocrates turned to the people of Somnolencia. "The real battle is not about sleep alone. It is about what we have been made to believe. It is time to reveal the lie they have fed us."

Madame Siesta stepped forward, tightening her blanket cape. "The lie that says you must always be doing something."

Captain Tosswell cracked his knuckles. "The lie that says rest is for the weak."

Sir Snoremore yawned deliberately, dramatically. "The lie… that says there is no time for dreams."

Hustlebane's expression darkened. "You tread dangerous ground, old man."

Zzzocrates laughed. "Then let us tread it together."

And thus, the people of Somnolencia prepared for their greatest battle yet, the battle to expose the Myth of Productivity.

The Cult of Productivity had come to claim their minds.

But Somnolencia?

Somnolencia was ready.

07

The Myth of Productivity

The Cult of Productivity had always lurked at the edges of Somnolencia, whispering their forbidden gospel of doing things to that unfortunate enough to listen. But now, emboldened by the stolen hour, they marched openly into the heart of the town, their pinstriped robes billowing, their spreadsheets clutched like sacred texts.

Overseer Hustlebane, their leader, stood tall atop a podium hastily erected in the town square. His suit shimmered with efficiency, his tie was so tight it could choke ambition into submission, and his watch never ticked late.

"Citizens of Somnolencia," he proclaimed, "you have been deceived."

A murmur spread through the weary crowd.

"The truth is simple," Hustlebane continued. "Your lethargy is a curse, your naps are chains, your idleness is a sickness. But worry not! We are here to show you a better way - a life of maximum output, a future where every moment is optimized for efficiency."

At this, his followers erupted into applause, though it was a measured, efficient clap, perfectly timed and evenly spaced.

Madame Siesta, wrapped in her ceremonial blanket, stepped forward. "A curse? A sickness? Listen here, you rigid relic of relentless routine! We Somnolencians know the truth: it is rest that fuels the soul."

Hustlebane smirked. "Ah, the comforting lie of the idle-minded. You fear work because you do not understand it."

Zzzocrates, standing beside her, adjusted his sleepy spectacles. "Oh, we understand work, Hustlebane. We simply reject the idea that it should consume our entire existence."

The crowd nodded. Even those who had been momentarily dazzled by the shiny schedules handed out by the cultists began to hesitate.

But Hustlebane was prepared. He raised a leather-bound tome high above his head, the Holy Manifesto of Productivity, its title gleaming in gold-embossed intimidation.

"The world rewards those who hustle," he declared. "Greatness is achieved through effort, perseverance, and sacrificing rest to push beyond one's limits!"

A few hesitant murmurs of agreement rippled through the crowd.

And then, Zzzocrates did something unthinkable.

He yawned. Loudly.

A collective gasp echoed through the square.

Lady Multitaska, standing beside Hustlebane, winced at the audacity of it. "Blasphemy," she hissed.

Zzzocrates stretched his arms lazily. "My dear Hustlebane, you stand before us, well-dressed and full of urgency, but you do not see the truth." He looked over the crowd and raised a silken finger. "You have been conditioned to believe that productivity equals worth. That if you are not doing something, you are failing."

Hustlebane scoffed. "Because it's true."

"No," Zzzocrates said, his voice steady. "It's a myth. A dangerous, exhausting myth designed to keep people running like hamsters in a wheel, never stopping to question why they're running in the first place."

The Cultists shifted uneasily. Some began clutching their planners a little tighter, doubt creeping into their restless eyes.

Zzzocrates turned to the crowd. "Do you remember the last time you felt truly rested?"

Silence.

Hustlebane's smirk faltered.

"Exactly," Zzzocrates said. "Because you've been convinced that you don't deserve rest. That slowing down means falling behind. That if you're not always grinding, always pushing, always achieving, then you're somehow less worthy."

He let the words settle, watching as the people of Somnolencia began to wake up - not from sleep, but from the illusion of endless work.

The Crack in the Cult's Armor

Even among the Cultists, some looked visibly shaken.

One of them - a nervous-looking man with a suit so stiff it could stand upright by itself, raised his hand hesitantly. "But… but I have a to-do list… If I don't finish it… then what was it all for?"

Zzzocrates approached him gently. "My friend, what has that list ever truly given you? Satisfaction? Joy? Peace?"

The man hesitated. "A sense of accomplishment?"

"And how long does that feeling last?" Zzzocrates asked.

The man blinked. "Until I have to make another list."

Zzzocrates nodded. "And that is the trap. The never-ending chase. The myth that the next achievement will finally bring peace. But it never does, does it?"

The man looked down at his leather-bound planner, uncertainty creeping into his features.

Even Hustlebane's unshakable confidence began to waver. He clenched his jaw. "This… this is nothing but dangerous rhetoric. If people stop working, if they stop moving, if they stop chasing goals"

"They start living," Zzzocrates finished.

And at that moment, something remarkable happened.

One of the Cultists collapsed.

Not in exhaustion, not in defeat but in sleep.

Another followed. Then another.

The most overworked, the most burnt-out, the ones who had spent years in perpetual motion, gave in.

They surrendered to the very thing they had been denying themselves.

Rest.

The Cult of Productivity was breaking.

Hustlebane's fists clenched. "This is not over."

He turned to Lady Multitaska, whose many arms were already flipping through several project reports at once. "We need to escalate," he muttered. "If they won't work willingly then we will force them into wakefulness."

Lady Multitaska smirked. "I think I know just the thing."

And with that, she pulled out a small vial filled with a swirling, electric-blue liquid.

"The solution is simple," she said, holding it up. "If they refuse to wake up, we will keep them awake forever."

The people of Somnolencia stared in horror.

Zzzocrates' eyes widened. "No… not that."

"Oh yes," Lady Multitaska purred.

08

The Arrival of the Forbidden Elixir

A storm of sleeplessness was about to sweep over Somnolencia.

At the heart of it stood Lady Multitaska, her many arms juggling ledgers, project reports, and steaming cups of liquid ambition. Beside her, Overseer Hustlebane watched with steely satisfaction as the first shipments of the dreaded elixir arrived in gleaming, industrial-sized barrels.

The vial she had revealed in the town square was but a small taste of what was to come. Now, before them, stood rows upon rows of bottled lightning - the most potent energy drink ever concocted.

They called it "VigoroMax: The Drink of the Tireless."

A single sip was said to banish drowsiness for hours. A full bottle? Days. And a whole case? Well, no one had ever lived to tell the tale, but it was rumoured that one poor soul had become so alert that he sensed the rotation of the planet itself and had to be strapped down to stop himself from running off the edge of the world.

Hustlebane grabbed a bottle and examined it. Its neon glow pulsed menacingly, almost alive. "This," he declared, "is how we win."

Lady Multitaska grinned. "Once they drink this, they will never sleep again."

And with that, the distribution began.

The First Tastes of Wakefulness

At first, the citizens of Somnolencia were suspicious.

Free samples of a mysterious drink? Given away by the Cult of Productivity? Surely, this was some kind of trick.

But then came the promises.

"Feeling drowsy? One sip, and you'll be as sharp as a sleepless sword!"

"Too many naps making you sluggish? Try VigoroMax! Get things done before sleep even notices you exist!"

"Side effects? None! Unless you consider extreme alertness, overwhelming focus, and mild reality distortion to be a bad thing!"

Slowly, temptation crept in.

The first to try it were the doubters, the ones who thought, Surely, it's just another gimmick. Nothing can overpower sleep.

They were wrong.

The moment the first drop touched their tongues, their pupils dilated, their breathing quickened, and their thoughts began moving at lightning speed.

"I… I CAN FINALLY FINISH EVERYTHING I STARTED," one exclaimed, twitching slightly.

Another clenched his fists. "I CAN FEEL TIME. I CAN SEE THE MOMENT BETWEEN MOMENTS."

A third blinked rapidly. "WHY HAVE I WASTED SO MUCH TIME SLEEPING?! I'M GONNA ORGANIZE EVERYTHING IN MY HOUSE RIGHT NOW!"

One by one, more Somnolencians fell to the temptation.

And so, the Great Insomnia Outbreak began.

The Unfolding Chaos

The once-lazy streets of Somnolencia were soon unrecognizable.

The Great Hammock Square? Empty.

The Nap Gardens? Trampled.

The famous Eternal Lounge, where generations had gathered to do absolutely nothing? Converted into a 24-hour co-working space.

People ran instead of walked. Conversations were fast and frantic. And worst of all, no one - absolutely no one was yawning.

Zzzocrates and Madame Siesta watched in horror.

"This… this is a catastrophe," Madame Siesta whispered, gripping her blanket staff. "They're becoming, productive."

Zzzocrates nodded grimly. "It's worse than that. They're becoming unstoppable."

They spotted one of their old friends, Dozer McDrift, a once-proud napper known for his ability to sleep through earthquakes. He was now pacing at a disturbing speed, holding seventeen different planners and muttering, "Deadlines… so many deadlines… must meet ALL expectations…"

Zzzocrates grabbed his shoulders. "Dozer! You have to fight it! You don't need to do all these things!"

Dozer jerked away. "YOU DON'T UNDERSTAND, ZZZOCRATES. I'M FINALLY UTILIZING MY FULL POTENTIAL. I'M…"

He twitched violently.

Then, with a horrifying snap, his body froze mid-motion, and he fell over, still awake.

"Oh no," Madame Siesta breathed.

Zzzocrates checked Dozer's pulse. His eyes were still open. He was still thinking. But his body had finally given out.

"If this continues," Zzzocrates muttered, his voice dark with dread, "they're all going to collapse."

And then, just as he feared, another fell. Then another.

The city was breaking down but not into the usual, blissful embrace of sleep. This was a restless paralysis, the body refusing to go on while the mind still raced at full speed.

It was a fate worse than exhaustion.

The Only Hope: The Science of Laziness

Madame Siesta turned to Zzzocrates, panic in her eyes. "What do we do?"

Zzzocrates took a deep breath. "We have to remind them of the truth. We have to show them the Science of Laziness."

She frowned. "But the Cult of Productivity has spent years convincing them that laziness is the enemy."

"Then it's time," Zzzocrates said, adjusting his sleepy spectacles, "to prove them wrong."

As more people collapsed under the weight of endless wakefulness, Zzzocrates turned to the remaining Somnolencians who had resisted.

"We need to prepare a counter argument. We must gather the oldest and laziest minds in Somnolencia. Those who have mastered the art of doing nothing. The sages who understand why rest is not just indulgence, but necessity."

Madame Siesta's eyes widened. "You mean… The Dreamers?"

Zzzocrates nodded solemnly. "Yes. The Dreamers of Old. The ones who hold the knowledge of deep rest, the art of true rejuvenation. They are the only ones who can undo this nightmare."

And so, as the world of Somnolencia teetered on the edge of permanent wakefulness, the last defenders of sleep set forth on a desperate mission:

To uncover the hidden science of laziness, before it was too late.

09

The Science of Laziness

Somnolencia was on the verge of collapse - but not into sleep.

The once-tranquil city now resembled a land of the restless, where the streets buzzed with jittery, over-caffeinated citizens locked in an endless loop of activity. The Great Hammock Square was deserted, the Nap Gardens lay in ruin, and the once-holy Pillow Sanctum had been converted into a Productivity Training Center by Sir Industrious' fanatics.

Those who had consumed the cursed energy elixir, VigoroMax, were trapped in a sleepless frenzy, their bodies screaming for rest while their minds remained flooded with an unnatural wakefulness.

Zzzocrates and Madame Siesta moved quickly through the streets, gathering the last remaining nappers, those who had resisted the pull of eternal motion.

"We don't have much time," Zzzocrates muttered, adjusting his sleepy spectacles.

Madame Siesta pulled her blanket cloak tightly around her shoulders. "How do we fight something that doesn't stop?

How do we convince them that doing nothing is sometimes the greatest thing one can do?"

Zzzocrates took a deep breath. "We use science."

Summoning the Dreamers

Their only hope lay with the Dreamers of Old - the keepers of Somnolencia's deepest knowledge, those who had unlocked the true potential of deliberate rest.

Deep within the Slumbering Archives, hidden beneath the ruins of the ancient Nap Temples, the Great Dozers rested.

Legends spoke of them as the last true masters of sleep, individuals who had reached such a perfect state of stillness that even time itself slowed around them.

And so, Zzzocrates and Madame Siesta descended into the darkness, stepping past the pillowy barriers of history, beyond the great Dozy Gates of Yawnheim - until they reached the Hall of Perpetual Slumber.

There, they found them.

Wrapped in sacred, enchanted blankets, the Dreamers lay in perfect repose - undisturbed for centuries, sustained by the very essence of deep rest.

It was said that in their slumber, they dreamt the future into existence.

Zzzocrates approached the Eldest Dreamer, a being so deeply at peace that his breath moved in harmony with the rhythm of the universe itself.

Zzzocrates knelt and whispered the ancient words:

"Awaken, O Dreamer. Somnolencia has need of you."

The Dreamer's eyelids fluttered. Slowly, he opened one eye.

"You have disturbed our rest," he murmured, his voice a soft sigh. "Speak, young one."

Zzzocrates wasted no time. "The people have fallen into wakefulness. A false belief has taken hold - one that says constant action is the key to progress. We must show them the truth."

The Eldest Dreamer closed his eye again, considering. Then, with a deep inhale, he stretched and the very air around him became lighter, as if the universe itself had just taken a long-overdue nap.

"The world has forgotten the Science of Laziness," the Dreamer said finally. "Then we shall teach them once more."

The Science of Doing Nothing (And Why It Matters)

The Dreamers emerged from their sanctuary and made their way to Napstone Plaza, where the sleepless masses trembled in exhaustion, yet refused to stop working.

Zzzocrates climbed atop a Great Beanbag Throne and addressed the people.

"You have been lied to," he began. "You have been told that busyness is worth more than rest. That to be still is to be wasteful. But I tell you this: Your bodies are failing because you have denied them their most sacred need - rejuvenation."

Murmurs spread through the crowd, but many still resisted.

"That's nonsense!" barked Overseer Hustlebane, one of Sir Industrious' top lieutenants. His eyes were bloodshot, his hands jittery from sleeplessness, but still, he refused to stop moving. "Work fuels progress! Laziness leads to ruin!"

Zzzocrates smirked. "Then tell me, dear Overseer, why do you look like a man about to collapse?"

Hustlebane's eye twitched.

Zzzocrates turned to the crowd.

"Sleep is not a weakness. Rest is not the enemy. The mind, the body, the very fabric of our souls - they thrive on balance. Do too much, and you burn out. Do too little, and you stagnate. But with just enough rest, one can achieve true clarity."

To prove his point, he gestured to the Dreamers of Old, who sat in perfect tranquillity, glowing with an otherworldly peace.

"These are the greatest minds in Somnolencia," Zzzocrates continued. "And they achieved their wisdom not through endless toil, but through the art of rest."

He turned back to Hustlebane. "Tell me, Overseer - who would you trust? A man on the edge of collapse, or a being so deeply rested that time bends around them?"

Hustlebane opened his mouth, but no words came out.

Because in that moment, his body finally betrayed him.

With a last, frantic twitch - he collapsed into a deep, desperate sleep.

The First Waves of Awakening

One by one, the others began to falter.

Workers stopped their frantic scribbling. Runners slowed their pace. Yawns - for the first time in days, began to spread like wildfire.

And then finally it happened.

A single soul, weary beyond belief, gave in to the inevitable.

They sat down.

Then another.

And another.

And then a miracle.

The first true nap in what felt like ages.

As one citizen slumped into their first restful sleep in days, the ripple effect was unstoppable. People collapsed into couches, fell onto pillows, and curled up wherever they stood.

Within minutes, half the city was asleep.

The energy drink's hold was breaking. The Science of Laziness had won.

Zzzocrates sighed in relief. "Finally," he whispered, "balance is restored."

But Madame Siesta was still troubled.

"Something isn't right," she murmured. "This was only the first battle."

Zzzocrates followed her gaze. Sir Industrious and Lady Multitaska were gone.

And deep beneath the ruins of the Productivity Engine, something stirred.

The Eternal Snooze Button (Why You Should Never Let Time Sleep for Too Long)

Zzzocrates turned to the Dreamers, who were once more preparing to return to their slumber.

"Wait," he said. "We need your wisdom once more. There is still a great battle ahead."

The Eldest Dreamer gave a knowing nod. "Yes," he murmured. "For beyond the realm of wakefulness, lies the realm of time itself."

And so, as Somnolencia drifted back into peace, a new mystery arose:

What ancient force lay beneath the Productivity Engine? And what powerful relic did Sir Industrious now seek?

There was only one answer.

The Eternal Snooze Button.

And if it fell into the wrong hands, time itself could be shattered.

10

The Eternal Snooze Button

Deep within the ruined halls of the Productivity Engine, beneath layers of broken gears and shattered timepieces, something pulsed with an eerie rhythm - a slow, steady beat that seemed to defy the very concept of urgency.

Zzzocrates, Madame Siesta, and the newly awakened Dreamers stood at the entrance of what was once the Heart of Industriousness, the inner sanctum where Sir Industrious had once drawn his power.

But that was not what troubled them now.

No, it was the relic that now lay exposed at the chamber's center, radiating a power both comforting and terrifying.

The Eternal Snooze Button.

A legendary artifact, spoken of only in whispers within the Pillow Prophecies.

It was said that whoever possessed the Snooze Button could control the very flow of time, bending it to their will - not by speeding it up, nor slowing it down, but by pausing it indefinitely.

In the wrong hands, it could freeze the world in an endless state of delay - an unbreakable cycle of "Just five more minutes" that could turn mere procrastination into eternal stagnation.

And now, the fate of Somnolencia hung upon who would claim it first.

The Race Against the Sleepless Tyrant

"Sir Industrious must not reach it before us," Madame Siesta said, pulling her blanket cloak tight around her shoulders.

Zzzocrates adjusted his sleepy spectacles. "Indeed. But I fear it may already be too late."

For as they stepped forward, a deep rumbling shook the ground beneath them.

The shadows at the far end of the hall shifted, and from the darkness emerged a familiar figure.

Sir Industrious.

And at his side, Lady Multitaska.

Her many arms juggled scrolls of endless schedules, lists of pending tasks, and the dreaded Clock of Perpetual Meetings, a cursed object that ensured no moment was ever free of obligation.

Her presence alone made the air feel urgent, the weight of responsibility pressing upon those who dared to relax.

"Well, well," Sir Industrious sneered. "You've arrived just in time to witness the dawn of a new era."

Lady Multitaska smirked, her hands flicking through productivity reports. "An era where time will never be wasted again."

Zzzocrates frowned. "Time is not wasted when used for rest. It is wasted when stolen by those who believe every moment must be filled with motion."

Sir Industrious' steel-plated boots clanked against the floor as he approached the relic. "The world has been held back by your laziness for too long, Zzzocrates. With the Eternal Snooze Button, I will finally put an end to delay and inefficiency."

Madame Siesta raised an eyebrow. "Oh? And how exactly do you plan to do that?"

Sir Industrious smirked. "Simple."

He raised his gauntleted hand and gestured toward the relic.

"I will press the Snooze Button, and I will lock all of time into an eternal workday."

A stunned silence filled the chamber.

Madame Siesta gasped. "You mean…"

"Yes." Sir Industrious' eyes glowed with fanaticism. "No more breaks. No more pauses. No more rest. Just a single, endless, waking moment of productivity."

Lady Multitaska cackled. "Imagine the efficiency! No wasted time! No delays! No interruptions! The world will never stop working!"

Zzzocrates adjusted his robe.

"And what happens when minds collapse from exhaustion? When bodies break under the weight of endless labour?"

Sir Industrious waved dismissively. "They will adapt."

Madame Siesta shook her head. "No, they will crumble."

Zzzocrates sighed. "You fool. You don't seek to control time - you seek to destroy balance."

He turned toward the Dreamers, whose presence had kept the natural rhythm of Somnolencia intact for centuries.

"Only the wise understand the true nature of time," Zzzocrates said. "It is not meant to be seized. It is meant to be respected."

Sir Industrious scoffed. "Words of a man who has wasted his years dreaming."

Madame Siesta stepped forward. "Then allow us to show you the power of dreams."

The Clash of Sleep and Wakefulness

At her signal, the Dreamers began to chant the Ancient Lullaby - a slow, rhythmic melody that pulled at the edges of reality itself.

Lady Multitaska's lists curled and crumpled in her hands, the ink smudging as if dissolving into dreams.

Sir Industrious stumbled, gripping his head as if fighting a powerful, invisible force.

"No," he growled. "I will not... I cannot..."

His resolve wavered - for even he was not immune to the pull of sleep.

But then, something unexpected happened.

The Eternal Snooze Button glowed brighter, as if awakening from its own slumber.

It pulsed - once, twice, and then, reality itself wobbled.

The Final Choice

A strange force gripped the room, freezing everyone in place.

The Button, it seemed, was offering a choice - a single press could pause time forever, trapping the world in a moment of either endless work or endless rest.

Both Sir Industrious and Zzzocrates hesitated.

One sought eternal motion.

The other sought balance.

It was now a battle of willpower - whoever reached the Button first would decide the fate of all time.

Sir Industrious lunged.

Zzzocrates reached out.

The Button flashed,

And then,

A hand slapped down on it.

But it was not Zzzocrates.

Nor Sir Industrious.

It was…

Madame Siesta.

A shockwave of pure, timeless energy rippled through the chamber, distorting everything - warping reality into a singularity of perfect stillness.

The Great Pause

The world froze.

For an instant - or was it eternity? Somnolencia stood on the edge of nonexistence.

But then,

The Button pulsed once more.

A new reality emerged - not one of endless work, nor one of eternal sleep, but one that respected both.

A world where the balance of time was restored.

As the glow faded, Zzzocrates exhaled. "She did it."

Sir Industrious fell to his knees, his strength drained. Lady Multitaska's schedules fluttered into dust, and the cursed Clock of Perpetual Meetings shattered.

Somnolencia had been saved.

Madame Siesta smiled, stepping back from the Button. "Time… deserves to breathe."

Zzzocrates turned to the people of Somnolencia, who were now awakening into a world where both work and rest had their place.

The battle was over.

But one final lesson remained.

The Philosophy of Doing Nothing.

11

The Philosophy of Doing Nothing (Why True Wisdom Lies in the Pause)

Somnolencia stood at the edge of transformation.

The war was over. Sir Industrious had fallen. Lady Multitaska's once-unbreakable schedules had turned to dust. The cursed Clock of Perpetual Meetings lay shattered, its relentless ticking finally silenced.

But as the dust settled, the citizens of Somnolencia faced a new question - what now?

They had fought to preserve rest, to protect their right to leisure and slowness. But what did it truly mean to embrace the philosophy of doing nothing?

Zzzocrates, now regarded as the Greatest Snooze Sage of All Time, gathered the weary yet victorious citizens in the heart of Slumberville. The air was thick with a strange mixture of relief and uncertainty.

"Now that the Productivity Engine is broken, should we still… do things?" one citizen hesitantly asked.

"Is it possible to do absolutely nothing forever?" another chimed in.

Zzzocrates smiled, adjusting his sleepy spectacles. "Ah, my dear Dreamers. The answer lies not in extremes, but in balance."

He turned toward the remnants of the Engine, its gears now lifeless, its once-intimidating presence reduced to an ornament of the past.

"Sir Industrious wanted to eliminate idleness. We resisted. But to reject all action entirely is to become lost in a different kind of trap."

The people murmured in thought. What, then, was the right way?

Zzzocrates chuckled. "Let me explain."

The Great Misunderstanding of Idleness

"Doing nothing is not about laziness," Zzzocrates said, settling into a particularly comfortable hammock that had been respectfully carried to him by the Sleepwalkers.

"Rather, it is about understanding that life is not meant to be a constant race."

He pointed to the ruins of Perpetuopolis in the distance. "Look at what happens when we treat time as something to be controlled. When we try to seize every second, when we force every moment to be filled with purpose, we destroy the very joy of living."

The Dreamers nodded, recalling the horror of Perpetual Productivity, the unrelenting march of wakefulness that had nearly consumed the world.

"But," Zzzocrates continued, wagging a sleepy finger, "rest without intention can lead to stagnation."

The Sleepwalkers murmured among themselves. Madame Siesta, wrapped in her legendary blanket cloak, nodded in agreement.

"To truly master the Art of Doing Nothing," Zzzocrates said, "one must understand the beauty of the pause."

The pause.

The space between effort and ease.

The moment when doing nothing is not neglect, but a choice.

The Great Pause: A World Rebalanced

Madame Siesta stepped forward. "We fought so hard to protect our right to rest. But true rest is not merely the absence of work. It is the presence of peace."

The citizens of Somnolencia felt a collective sigh ripple through their souls.

For too long, they had feared that productivity was an enemy. But now they saw the truth - productivity itself was not the villain.

It was compulsion, urgency, the fear of stopping.

They did not need to reject action entirely. They simply needed to remember that pausing was sacred.

The Birth of the Order of Stillness

And so, a new movement began in Somnolencia - The Order of Stillness.

Its members, known as The Practitioners of the Pause, dedicated themselves to mastering the art of restful existence.

Their teachings included:

The Power of the Nap – A sacred practice that strengthened both mind and spirit.

The Meditation of the Unfinished Task – The wisdom of leaving things undone without guilt.

The Ritual of the Blank Calendar – The divine act of not over-scheduling oneself.

Zzzocrates, as the first Grandmaster of the Order, left one final lesson:

"True wisdom is found not in constant action, nor in absolute stillness, but in the pause between them."

And as the people embraced their new way of life, a great celebration was planned - The Festival of the Sacred Yawn.

It would be a time for all to come together, stretch, sigh contentedly, and share stories of their finest naps.

Somnolencia was at peace once more.

But beyond its borders, a new challenge was rising.

For even as Somnolencia embraced balance, rumours were spreading of a new movement - one that sought to take relaxation to an extreme.

A philosophy so radical that even Zzzocrates himself felt a shiver of unease.

It was whispered only in the deepest corners of drowsy minds.

A secret doctrine that claimed:

Doing nothing was not merely a practice but an art form.

12

Why Doing Nothing is an Art Form

In the quiet streets of Somnolencia, where hammocks swayed in the warm breeze and pillows were considered national treasures, a new thought began to take root.

For generations, the people of Somnolencia had fought against the tyranny of endless toil, the relentless pursuit of efficiency, and the horrors of scheduled wakefulness. They had won their right to rest, but now, a deeper question arose.

Was mere idleness enough?

Or was doing nothing itself an art form, something that had to be understood, refined, and mastered?

Zzzocrates, the newly anointed Grandmaster of the Order of Stillness, had long pondered this question. He had already established the teachings of The Great Pause, guiding the citizens toward a life of restful balance.

But there were whispers, strange rumours that troubled even him.

There were those who believed that true idleness was not just a practice but a divine state, an untapped potential far beyond mere napping.

And if this power were to be misused, Somnolencia could face an entirely new kind of crisis.

The Rise of the Extreme Idlers

It began subtly at first.

A group of devoted dreamers started calling themselves The Masters of Absolute Stillness.

They did not merely nap.

They did not simply rest.

They sought a higher level of doing nothing, an existence where even thought was a distraction, where even blinking was an unnecessary effort.

They studied the ancient Scrolls of the Dozing Sage, deciphering lost texts that spoke of The Ultimate Recline, a technique so powerful that those who mastered it could supposedly enter a state of perpetual slumber while remaining fully aware.

The Sleepwalkers, who had long embraced lucid dreaming as a way of life, were intrigued - but wary.

If the Practitioners of the Pause sought balance, the Masters of Absolute Stillness sought absolute surrender to idleness.

They called it The Final Nap.

And they believed that only by embracing total stillness could one reach the pinnacle of relaxation.

This was no longer about resisting productivity.

This was about transcending existence itself.

The Warning of Zzzocrates

Zzzocrates, though the greatest defender of Somnolent Philosophy, felt uneasy.

"Idleness is an art," he reminded his followers, "but art requires awareness. A painter does not become great by merely holding a brush and never using it. A dreamer does not shape their world by simply closing their eyes and fading away."

His words were wise, but the Masters of Absolute Stillness were undeterred.

They claimed that Zzzocrates, for all his wisdom, had only scratched the surface of true rest.

They declared that The Final Nap was the ultimate rebellion against wakefulness, the purest form of defiance against the horrors of the past.

And so, they prepared.

A grand event was planned - an unprecedented gathering of idlers to showcase the many forms of doing nothing.

It was to be called…

The First Ever Festival of Idleness.

But deep within his heart, Zzzocrates knew, this festival would be more than just a celebration.

It would be a test.

And if the people of Somnolencia failed, they might never wake up again.

13

The First Ever Festival of Idleness (the Nap That Went Too Far)

The people of Somnolencia had gathered in Snore Square, the heart of the land's napping culture, where pillows lined the streets, and hammocks swayed lazily between golden Dreamwood trees.

A grand event was about to unfold - the First Ever Festival of Idleness, a celebration of supreme relaxation, artful lounging, and the pursuit of perfect stillness.

This was no ordinary gathering.

The festival would bring together every faction of the idle world - from the Deep Dreamers, who could drift into sleep at will, to the Midday Recliners, who specialized in the art of strategic naps. Even the Yawning Monks of the Dozing Hills, known for their centuries-old technique of continuous restfulness, had agreed to participate.

But among them, the most anticipated group was the Masters of Absolute Stillness.

These devotees of The Final Nap believed that true enlightenment lay in total inactivity - an existence so effortless, so immobile, that it teetered on the edge of complete unconsciousness.

The event's grand attraction was set to be The Great Slumber-Off, where the most skilled idlers would compete to see who could remain in the deepest, most undisturbed rest for the longest period.

Some saw it as a friendly competition.

Others saw it as a dangerous experiment.

And as Zzzocrates looked upon the gathering crowd, he felt an unease settle in his chest.

He knew, deep in his bones, that this festival would not end as planned.

The Great Slumber-Off Begins

The rules were simple.

The contestants had to remain perfectly still, perfectly at peace, for as long as possible.

Some sank into pillowed nests, others curled into weighted-blanket cocoons, and the most extreme competitors - those devoted to The Final Nap - entered a state of near-hibernation, their breathing slowing to a whisper, their limbs unmoving.

Time passed.

Hours.

Then days.

Some participants succumbed to hunger and rolled out of their beds, disqualified. Others fell asleep so deeply that they forgot they were even competing.

But a select few remained - frozen in place, lost in a realm of boundless stillness.

At first, it was a marvel.

The people of Somnolencia cheered, in the softest, most non-disruptive manner possible.

But then… something changed.

The Nap That Went Too Far

The Masters of Absolute Stillness had reached a level of immobility that defied nature.

Their stillness was too perfect, their bodies too relaxed.

A hush fell over the crowd.

Even Zzzocrates, who had witnessed the greatest sleepers in history, felt a chill crawl up his spine.

"They've… gone too far," he murmured.

The onlookers began to murmur among themselves.

Were they even breathing?

Could they be awakened?

As concern grew, the Sleepwalkers - masters of guiding others through the dream realm - attempted to nudge their consciousness back to life.

Nothing.

The Masters of Absolute Stillness had entered a sleep so deep, so utterly devoid of movement, that they had crossed a threshold no one had dared approach before.

They were…

Stuck.

Trapped in The Final Nap.

Panic surged through the festival.

This was supposed to be a celebration of idleness, not a descent into the abyss of unconsciousness!

Zzzocrates rushed forward, his mind racing.

The people of Somnolencia were masters of rest, but never before had they faced the challenge of awakening those who no longer wished to wake.

And as he stood before the frozen dreamers, he realized something else -

This was no longer just about sleep.

This was about the true limits of stillness itself.

The people of Somnolencia had spent centuries perfecting the art of doing nothing, but had they finally found the one thing that even they could not undo?

The festival of idleness had given birth to a new, terrifying question -

If sleep is an art, then when does it stop being restful, and start becoming a trap?

And with that, the people of Somnolencia knew what had to come next.

A challenge unlike any other.

A test of balance, movement, and the very essence of relaxation itself.

It was time for…

The Challenge of Stillness.

14

The Challenge of Stillness

The Festival of Idleness had ended in unease.

Where there should have been celebration and drowsy satisfaction, there was only whispers of dread.

The Masters of Absolute Stillness - those who had gone too far, remained motionless, lost in a sleep so deep, so perfect, that they seemed beyond reach.

At first, the people of Somnolencia marvelled at their achievement.

Then they feared it.

For the first time in history, a question that had never before needed asking was now on everyone's lips:

Can one rest too much?

If sleep was supposed to restore and rejuvenate, why did these motionless figures seem so lifeless?

Zzzocrates, the wisest of all Sleep Scholars, was the first to admit it:

"We have reached the threshold of sleep itself. If we do not understand its limits, we risk falling into a slumber from which even dreams cannot return."

And thus, the Challenge of Stillness was born.

A test, not of how long one could rest, but of how to balance rest and wakefulness, stillness and movement, idleness and action.

It was time for Somnolencia to confront its greatest paradox.

The land of perfect rest had never been so restless.

The Trial of Balance Begins

To understand the delicate equilibrium between stillness and motion, the Council of Naps convened an emergency summit in Yawnhalla, the great slumbering hall where all matters of drowsy diplomacy were decided.

The wisest minds of Somnolencia gathered:

Grandmaster Drowzeus, philosopher of naps, whose ability to doze mid-sentence was unmatched.

Snorlock the Sage, who had studied the fine art of productive procrastination.

Lady Multitaska, the only citizen who had once tried to be both active and inactive at the same time, causing a metaphysical paradox that no one dared to revisit.

The Napwalkers, guardians of the sacred Dream-Veil, who had long understood that sleep was not merely absence, but an ever-shifting state between worlds.

Together, they crafted The Trial of Balance - a series of tests meant to explore the dangers of too much stillness and too much motion.

Three groups of volunteers were chosen.

The Deep Dreamers, who would attempt to wake the frozen slumberers.

The Idle Extremists, who would test just how much stillness the body could endure before it became dangerous.

The Sleepwalkers, who would try to understand what happened when motion and sleep coexisted.

Each group had its own challenge, but the most feared of all was the Final Test.

Could they wake those who had gone too far?

The Crisis of the Frozen Dreamers

The first attempts were simple.

Gentle nudges.

Soft lullabies played in reverse.

The scent of fresh morning coffee (a forbidden relic in Somnolencia, but desperate times called for desperate measures).

Nothing worked.

The Masters of Absolute Stillness remained trapped.

It was then that Lady Multitaska made an observation that sent a chill through the council.

"They are still dreaming," she said, pointing to their closed eyes.

"What?" Zzzocrates blinked. "How can you tell?"

She knelt beside one of the frozen dreamers, carefully observing the faintest flicker beneath their eyelids.

"Their minds are not empty. They are moving, but only within."

That changed everything.

These dreamers were not lost to nothingness - they were trapped in a world of endless dreams, unable to wake.

And if they could not wake, what separated them from the restless spirits of Perpetuopolis?

What if… they were already ghosts in a world of their own making?

The room fell into an uneasy silence.

The Challenge of Motion

Meanwhile, the Idle Extremists were testing the opposite end of the spectrum.

How still was too still?

The answer came shockingly fast.

For as long as they remained motionless, they felt peaceful, calm, and deeply rested.

But then…

They began to experience something else.

Their bodies refused to move.

Their thoughts became slow.

A strange, eerie silence overtook them.

And just as Lady Multitaska had feared, some of them began to see things in the corners of their vision.

Whispers.

Faint figures standing at the edge of reality.

It was the same phenomenon that had plagued Perpetuopolis - the first sign of being lost to the sleep beyond sleep.

The boundary between rest and oblivion was thinner than they had ever imagined.

Zzzocrates knew now -

Stillness was not the answer.

It had to be balanced with movement.

Even in a land built on naps and idleness, too much of one thing could be dangerous.

And as the council reconvened, they realized something even more alarming.

The Masters of Absolute Stillness were not alone in their sleep.

Forces unseen were moving.

And they were about to witness a phenomenon that had never occurred in Somnolencia before.

Something… was waking up.

And it was moving against its will.

15

The Mysterious Case of Unwanted Movement

For a land that prided itself on the mastery of idleness, movement - especially uninvited movement - was a most unnerving phenomenon.

And yet, as the Council of Naps debated the fate of the Frozen Dreamers, something strange was happening.

At first, it was subtle.

A slight twitch of a sleeping hand.

A barely perceptible shudder in a motionless figure.

A toe curling, despite its owner being deep in slumber.

But then... it escalated.

The dreamers who had been lost in Absolute Stillness, who had remained motionless for weeks, began to stir.

And not in the way someone naturally wakes from a nap.

No...

These movements were unnatural.

Jerky, disjointed, and mechanical.

As if some unseen force was pulling at them, shifting their limbs against their will.

The Silent Awakening

Zzzocrates, Snorlock the Sage, and Lady Multitaska were the first to witness the full extent of the phenomenon.

It was past midnight when they gathered in the Chamber of Eternal Repose, the sacred resting hall where the motionless dreamers lay.

A thick drowsy mist hovered over the room.

The only sound was the occasional deep sigh of sleep.

And then -

A gasp.

Lady Multitaska nearly jumped out of her robes as one of the frozen dreamers sat upright -their eyes still shut; their body still lost in sleep.

Zzzocrates grabbed his sleeping cap in alarm.

Snorlock squinted, rubbing his own half-lidded eyes.

"Did… did they just wake up?"

"No," Lady Multitaska whispered, her hands trembling. "They're still dreaming."

One by one, more motionless figures began to move.

Some slowly sat up. Others jerked their limbs as if tangled in invisible strings.

They were not waking up - they were being woken up.

Something was pulling them back to the waking world… against their will.

The Return of the Sleepwalkers

A voice from the doorway interrupted their horrified silence.

"This is no natural waking," said Professor Hypnagog, the legendary scholar of dream physics.

His long, flowing nightgown trailed behind him as he shuffled into the chamber.

"This…" he said, pointing a trembling hand at the rising figures, "is a breach in the Dream-Veil."

The room fell silent.

Everyone knew the Dream-Veil, the delicate barrier between sleep and wakefulness.

It was the force that allowed Somnolencia's people to remain peacefully at rest without accidentally drifting into the abyss of perpetual wakefulness (a fate too horrible to contemplate).

But the Dream-Veil was never meant to be torn.

And yet…

These sleep-trapped dreamers were being dragged back into wakefulness, their bodies rebelling against their perfect rest.

"Someone," Professor Hypnagog said grimly, "is forcing them awake."

Zzzocrates's face darkened. "Only one mind in existence would dare commit such an atrocity."

Lady Multitaska clenched her fists. "Sir Industrious."

A collective shudder passed through the council.

Hadn't he been defeated? Hadn't Perpetuopolis fallen?

Snorlock shook his head. "If this is his doing, then we were fools to think the war was over."

Because if Sir Industrious had truly returned, it meant one thing:

He had found a way to infiltrate the world of sleep itself.

And now, he was pulling the dreamers into his domain.

The Fear of the Restless Curse

The implications were terrifying.

If these dreamers woke against their will, they would be lost forever to the waking world, unable to find their way back to the peaceful embrace of slumber.

A fate worse than mere sleeplessness.

A life of endless, inescapable wakefulness.

It was a curse that had long been theorized but never before witnessed - The Restless Curse.

And if Sir Industrious had discovered how to force people into it.

Then the very foundation of Somnolencia was under attack.

The Great Nap was no longer just under threat - it was unravelling.

A Desperate Attempt to Stop the Awakening

"We have to act now," Lady Multitaska said urgently.

But how?

How did one fight against forced wakefulness?

Zzzocrates, deep in thought, stroked his fluffy sleep-beard.

Then, an idea struck him.

"The only way to resist unnatural waking…" he murmured, "is to dive even deeper into sleep."

Lady Multitaska frowned. "You mean?"

"Yes."

It was the oldest and most dangerous method ever recorded.

A technique so powerful it had only been attempted once before - during the Age of Endless Yawning.

Zzzocrates turned to the council, his eyes heavy with both wisdom and exhaustion.

"We must attempt The Great Attempt."

A stunned silence followed.

The Great Attempt - a descent into the deepest realms of sleep - a place so profound, so undisturbed, that even the forces of wakefulness could not reach it.

It was a gamble. A risky and terrifying one.

Because if they failed, the dreamers wouldn't just wake up, they might never return.

But they had no choice.

Sir Industrious was ripping their people from slumber.

And if they did not act now, the world of sleep would soon be no more.

16

The Great Attempt

The Council of Naps sat in stunned silence as Zzzocrates' words hung in the air.

The Great Attempt.

It was forbidden lore, a technique so radical that only one dreamer in all of Somnolencia's history had ever attempted it - The Dozing Sage, whose fate remained a mystery lost to the deepest layers of slumber.

Lady Multitaska's eyes darted from one council member to another. "Are we truly prepared for this?"

Snorlock the Sage, normally composed, let out a deep sigh. "If Sir Industrious has found a way to pull us from our dreams, then we have no choice."

Professor Hypnagog nodded gravely. "Only by diving into the deepest possible sleep - deeper than even the Dream-Veil itself, can we escape his reach."

A murmur of unease rippled through the chamber.

Even the Sleepwalkers, those trapped between sleep and wakefulness, hesitated.

For the Great Attempt was not just about sleeping deeply.

It was about surrendering completely.

And there was no guarantee of return.

The Preparation for the Descent

The ritual was ancient, its steps recorded only in whispers within The Pillow Prophecies.

The Council gathered at the Pillow Sanctum, a vast chamber lined with cloud-soft cushions and blankets woven from the dreams of the drowsiest sages.

Each participant was given a Cup of Midnight, a mystical tea brewed from the rarest Moonflowers of Lethargis, known to induce near-eternal drowsiness.

Zzzocrates raised his cup. "Once we drink this, our bodies will enter The Untouched Realm - the deepest level of sleep ever known."

Lady Multitaska hesitated. "And if we don't wake up?"

Zzzocrates' face was unreadable. "Then we will dream forever."

A long silence followed.

Then, one by one, they drank.

The Descent into The Deepest Sleep

It began slowly - a heaviness settling over them like a thousand warm blankets.

Their minds drifted beyond the realms of ordinary slumber.

Through the first layer, the Dreamer's Meadow, where half-formed dreams wandered aimlessly.

Through the second layer, the Lullaby Sea, where the waves hummed songs that could put even the most restless minds into a trance.

Through the third layer, the Horizon of Forgetting, where sleepers lost all sense of time and self.

And then…

They crossed the Dream-Veil.

Deeper.

Deeper.

Even deeper.

Until they arrived at a place few had ever reached.

A place where even dreams dared not stir.

The Untouched Realm.

The Land of Forgotten Sleep

They floated in an infinite stillness, a place beyond time, beyond thought.

Here, no alarms could ring. No responsibilities could intrude.

It was perfect peace.

But something was wrong.

In the distance, a shadow moved.

Lady Multitaska tried to speak, but no words came.

Zzzocrates' eyes widened.

It was not Sir Industrious.

It was something older.

Something that had been waiting here since the first dreamer closed their eyes.

A Voice from the Abyss

A deep resonant voice echoed through the stillness.

"You have come too far."

The sleepers shuddered.

Before them stood a figure cloaked in an endless night, its form shifting like the space between dreams.

Zzzocrates' breath caught.

"The Ultimate Visitor."

The Guardian of the Final Dream.

The one entity that even the sleep sages feared.

For no one who had met The Ultimate Visitor had ever returned.

And now, it was staring directly at them.

17

The Ultimate Visitor

In the deepest corners of the Untouched Realm, where even nightmares feared to tread, the Council of Naps stood frozen.

Before them loomed a figure of infinite stillness, draped in a cloak woven from the darkest moments of slumber, its presence as heavy as the weight of unspent exhaustion.

It had no face, only an endless void where the mind longed to wander yet feared to fall.

"The Ultimate Visitor," whispered Zzzocrates, his voice barely more than an exhale.

The Guardian of the Final Dream.

The One Who Waits at the Edge of Sleep.

Lady Multitaska, for once in her life, had no words.

Even Sir Snorlock, who had mastered the art of sleep-talking, could not utter a sound.

The figure tilted its head slightly, as though peering into their very souls.

"You are not meant to be here," it murmured, its voice layered with the whispers of countless forgotten dreamers.

The Warning

The air grew thicker, pressing down upon them like a blanket too heavy to lift.

"You have ventured beyond the Dream-Veil," The Ultimate Visitor continued, "and now you stand at the threshold of The Final Sleep."

Zzzocrates took a hesitant step forward. "We seek a way to defeat Sir Industrious - to reclaim our right to slumber. We thought… perhaps… the answer lay here."

The figure remained motionless.

"Sleep and Wakefulness are forces that must remain in balance," it intoned. "Yet you seek to plunge ever deeper, while another seeks to drag the world to its feet."

A silence settled over them, heavier than any before.

Then a flicker of movement within the void of the Visitor's form.

From its cloak, a glimmering object emerged - a perfect, unmarked hourglass, filled with neither sand nor time.

"The fate of the world hangs on a single thread," The Ultimate Visitor said. "But before you may reclaim your path, you must answer one question."

The hourglass tilted forward, and in the reflection of its glass, they saw something terrifying -

Not the future.

Not the past.

But a vision of a world where time itself had ceased to move.

An eternal pause.

A sleep without waking.

A stillness that would never end.

Lady Multitaska gasped. "That's… that's not what we wanted."

Zzzocrates clenched his fists. "What is this? A warning?"

The Visitor's voice echoed one last time.

"An answer to a question you did not know to ask."

Then -

Darkness.

And then -

A sudden, jarring noise.

A blaring, shrill sound that sent their entire consciousness spiralling back toward wakefulness.

An alarm.

Not just any alarm.

The Alarm.

The one that had been forbidden in Somnolencia for centuries.

Awakening in Chaos

The Council awoke with a gasp, jolted from the Untouched Realm, back into the heart of Somnolencia.

The once calm city of Slumberville was in disarray.

People ran through the streets, covering their ears, their dreams shattered.

The ancient alarms of Perpetuopolis - Sir Industrious' greatest weapon had been unleashed.

And now, all of Somnolencia was waking up.

Zzzocrates looked at the others. "We have to stop it. Before it's too late."

Lady Multitaska's face was pale. "But how? The alarm is everywhere."

Professor Hypnagog's eyes widened in horror.

"We may not have a choice," he whispered. "We may have to do the unthinkable."

The council turned to him, dread settling in.

"The Alarming Suggestion."

18

The Alarming Suggestion

The air in Somnolencia trembled under the relentless, shrill assault of The Alarm - a piercing, unnatural wail that burrowed into the minds of dreamers like a merciless drill.

Citizens clutched their pillows in agony, some trying to muffle their ears, others staggering in confusion, their dreams shattered beyond repair.

Sir Snorlock was on his knees, eyes wide with disbelief.

"This is… monstrous," he whispered, voice nearly lost in the chaos.

Lady Multitaska, usually unfazed, had her fingers jammed into her ears, her face twisted in panic.

Zzzocrates, barely holding on to his sanity, turned to Professor Hypnagog.

"We need to stop this. Now."

The Professor, though visibly shaken, took a deep breath.

"There is… one way," he said.

The others turned to him with desperate hope.

Then -

He hesitated.

His fingers twitched. His mouth opened, but no words came out.

Lady Multitaska grabbed him by the shoulders, shaking him. "Spit it out! Before I lose my last remaining nap schedule!"

The Professor gulped. Then, slowly -

He uttered the words that would shake the foundation of Somnolencia itself.

"The only way to stop The Alarm… is to set off another one."

The Unspeakable Plan

A horrified silence fell upon the council.

Zzzocrates paled. "You're saying we fight one alarm with… another alarm?"

"Yes," Hypnagog nodded grimly. "We use the Counter-Disturbance Resonance Effect."

Sir Snorlock's Mustache quivered. "The… the, what now?"

"The Science of Sleep Disruption states that if one irritating noise is played at an exact opposite frequency of another"

Lady Multitaska's eyes widened. "They cancel each other out!"

"Exactly."

For a moment, hope flickered in the exhausted council's eyes.

Then, realization dawned.

Zzzocrates groaned. "But that means…"

Lady Multitaska gasped.

Sir Snorlock collapsed onto a beanbag.

Professor Hypnagog nodded grimly.

"Yes."

"To save Somnolencia, we must activate the Legendary Snooze Alarm."

The Most Forbidden Device in All of Somnolencia

A collective shudder passed through the council.

The Legendary Snooze Alarm was no ordinary alarm.

It was the only alarm designed to instantly override wakefulness itself.

It was an ancient relic, buried deep beneath the Hall of Eternal Drowsiness, rumoured to be so powerful that if triggered, it could cause the entire universe to question whether it should wake up at all.

And for centuries, it had remained untouched, locked away for fear of what it might unleash.

Lady Multitaska ran a hand through her stress-matted hair.

"I thought it was a myth."

Zzzocrates nodded. "It is. But all myths start somewhere."

Professor Hypnagog took a deep breath. "Then we must unearth it. Before The Alarm drives us all into the madness of wakefulness."

Sir Snorlock groaned. "I never thought I'd say this, but I think I need a nap just to prepare for this."

"Too late for that," Zzzocrates muttered, adjusting his robes. "We move now."

With that, the Council of Naps rose from their beanbags, their eyes set on the forgotten chambers beneath the city.

And deep below Somnolencia, in the sealed vault of sleep itself, something stirred.

Something that had not been disturbed for an eternity.

Something that had been waiting.

For the right moment.

For the right dreamers.

For the Rebellion of Sorts.

19

Rebellion of Sorts

Deep beneath Somnolencia, the chamber of the Legendary Snooze Alarm had remained sealed for centuries, its very existence known only to the oldest and drowsiest of scholars.

Now, as the Council of Naps approached its forbidden entrance, the air itself felt heavier, infused with a dreamlike stillness.

Zzzocrates placed a hand on the ancient stone doors, tracing the carvings of pillows, blankets, and the sacred yawn.

"We're about to break every rule of responsible napping," he murmured.

Lady Multitaska, ever restless, tapped her foot impatiently. "Then let's do it already. Every second we hesitate, The Alarm grows stronger."

Sir Snorlock sighed. "I never thought I'd see the day when an actual rebellion would take place in Somnolencia."

Professor Hypnagog nodded solemnly. "It was only a matter of time. The tyranny of wakefulness can push even the laziest to action."

With a deep breath, Zzzocrates pushed the doors open.

Inside, the Legendary Snooze Alarm awaited.

The Most Dangerous Nap Ever Taken

At first glance, the Snooze Alarm was underwhelming - a small, round button resting on a plush velvet cushion, surrounded by dimly glowing hourglasses.

But the closer they got, the heavier their eyelids became.

Sir Snorlock swayed. "I… I suddenly feel the need… to rest…"

Professor Hypnagog snapped his fingers. "Of course! The Snooze Alarm doesn't just stop wakefulness, it ensnares reality itself in a perpetual cycle of half-sleep."

Lady Multitaska shook her head, struggling to stay upright. "If we're going to use this thing, we need a way to control it. Otherwise, we'll all end up stuck in an eternal drowsy limbo."

Zzzocrates studied the inscriptions, his scholar's mind racing.

"There is… one way." He hesitated. "But it's dangerous."

"Spit it out," Lady Multitaska snapped.

"We need to volunteer someone to press the button and resist the sleep it induces for just long enough to wake us all up at the right moment."

A horrified silence fell over the group.

Sir Snorlock frowned. "That sounds… absurdly difficult."

Professor Hypnagog sighed. "It is. A battle between sleep and wakefulness, fought within the very mind of the dreamer."

Lady Multitaska crossed her arms. "Who in their right mind would agree to that?"

Zzzocrates stepped forward.

"I will."

The council stared at him.

Lady Multitaska's mouth fell open. "You? The oldest, drowsiest, most nap-prone philosopher in all of Somnolencia?"

Zzzocrates gave a small, sleepy smile.

"Yes. Because only someone who truly understands the value of sleep can resist it when it matters most."

Sir Snorlock wiped a tear from his eye. "That's… beautiful."

Professor Hypnagog adjusted his glasses. "Foolish, but beautiful."

Lady Multitaska shook her head. "Then let's get this over with."

Zzzocrates stepped forward, reaching out -

And pressed the Legendary Snooze Alarm.

The Ripple Through Reality

The moment his hand made contact, a pulse of sleep magic erupted from the button, washing over Somnolencia like a slow-moving tide of comfort, warmth, and absolute drowsiness.

The Alarm - the horrifying, jarring wail that had plagued them began to distort.

It flickered.

It wobbled.

And then,

For the first time in what felt like eternity -

It stopped.

Silence.

Glorious, restful silence.

Across Somnolencia, citizens collapsed into their beds, their beanbags, their piles of impossibly soft blankets.

Even Sir Industrious' forces staggered, their militant rigidity faltering as yawns spread like wildfire through their ranks.

The rebellion had begun.

The sleepers were fighting back - not with force, but with a defiant return to true rest.

But deep within his mind, Zzzocrates fought a battle of his own.

Because he had pressed the button.

And now, the Snooze Alarm was trying to claim him forever.

20

The Call to Action

Deep in the realm of half-sleep, Zzzocrates floated between awareness and oblivion, caught in the vast, uncharted dreamscape of the Legendary Snooze Alarm.

He could hear the voices of his companions fading in and out, like echoes from another world.

"You have to wake up, Zzzocrates!"

"If you don't, we're all doomed to an eternity of… of… of…"

Silence.

Had they already drifted into slumber?

Zzzocrates could feel the weight of sleep pressing down on him, a comforting, endless void pulling him deeper.

This was, after all, the very essence of true rest.

Would it be so terrible to surrender?

But then -

A distant sound.

A beeping noise.

Faint at first but growing louder.

The Alarm was returning.

Zzzocrates forced his eyes open, struggling against the pull of sleep.

No.

He had pressed the Snooze Button to silence the tyranny of forced wakefulness, but that didn't mean Somnolencia could sleep forever.

They needed balance.

They needed one final push -

A call to action.

A Yawn Heard Across Somnolencia

Back in the physical world, the Council of Naps stood anxiously around Zzzocrates' still form.

His body remained motionless, except for a small, rhythmic movement -

The rising and falling of his chest.

"He's still breathing," muttered Sir Snorlock. "But he's… too deep. If he doesn't come back soon, we'll all be lost."

Lady Multitaska, pacing furiously, snapped her fingers. "We need to rally the dreamers. If we can't wake him, we'll wake the world."

Professor Hypnagog adjusted his glasses. "And how do you propose we do that? A battle cry? A trumpet blast?"

Lady Multitaska smirked.

"Something stronger."

She turned toward Somnolencia's Grand Balcony, where the leaders of the drowsy realm once delivered their most profound wisdom - usually in the form of bedtime stories.

She took a deep breath.

And then,

She yawned.

Loudly.

Gloriously.

A yawn so powerful, so contagious, it swept across the entire city like a wave of exhaustion.

People turned, one by one, as the yawn spread.

Within minutes, the effect reached the outer edges of Somnolencia, rolling through the streets, slipping into bedrooms, pulling even the most restless into its grasp.

Even Sir Industrious' forces - those who had resisted the call of sleep for so long felt their eyelids droop.

The tyranny of busyness was cracking.

But would it be enough?

The Final Awakening

In the depths of his mind, Zzzocrates felt it.

The yawn.

A force more powerful than any alarm, any schedule, any system of forced labour.

His fingers twitched.

His breath quickened.

And then,

He opened his eyes.

For the first time in ages, he was awake.

And as he sat up, blinking, he saw what he had set in motion.

All around him, the people of Somnolencia were rising from their beds, stretching, blinking away the fog of eternal sleep.

But they weren't waking into the world of Industrious' making.

No - this was something new.

Something balanced.

A world where wakefulness and rest coexisted in perfect harmony.

A world on the brink of its final victory.

Because the next step was inevitable.

The next step was the Fall of Busyness.

The Fall of Busyness (How Productivity Finally Faced Its Reckoning)

For the first time in countless cycles, the clocks of Perpetuopolis stopped ticking.

The gears of the Efficiency Engine, once the driving force behind Sir Industrious' empire, ground to a halt with an almost satisfying sigh.

Across the former strongholds of industry, workers who had spent years trapped in the ceaseless churn of productivity did something unthinkable -

They sat down.

Some stretched.

Some yawned.

Some curled up right where they stood, napping on the factory floors.

The world had been running on borrowed time, pushing forward at an impossible pace, and now -

It had finally collapsed under its own weight.

And as the final remnants of Sir Industrious' rule crumbled, a new realization swept across the land:

Work, for the sake of work, had no meaning.

The citizens of Perpetuopolis looked to Somnolencia, not as an enemy, but as a model of balance.

A place where rest was not laziness, but wisdom.

And yet -

Something unexpected was beginning to stir.

The Dangers of an Empty Schedule

In the wake of The Great Slowdown, something strange began to happen.

At first, it was subtle.

People, freed from their burdens, rejoiced.

They basked in their newfound idleness, reclaimed their stolen naps, and sank into their comfiest beds.

But as days passed, a creeping sense of aimlessness set in.

Without the oppressive weight of productivity, some found themselves adrift, uncertain of what to do.

The question that had haunted the people of Perpetuopolis before - "How can I get more done?" had been replaced with something even more unsettling:

"Now that I can rest, what do I do with all this time?"

It was in this moment of uncertainty that a new movement began to take shape.

A new philosophy, born not out of struggle, but out of absolute inertia.

It began with a whisper.

A murmur among the drowsiest corners of Somnolencia.

Then it grew.

A new way of life was on the horizon.

Not the mindless hustle of Sir Industrious.

Not the balanced harmony Zzzocrates had envisioned.

No - this was something else entirely.

It was passive laziness.

A state where nothing was done.

Ever.

Where decisions were avoided, actions were delayed indefinitely, and the mere thought of doing anything at all became exhausting.

Was this the natural conclusion of the struggle?

Had the people fought so hard for their right to rest, only to become trapped in an endless cycle of indecision and apathy?

Zzzocrates felt a chill run through him.

They had toppled the empire of busyness, but had they gone too far?

The next battle wouldn't be fought against an external enemy.

It would be fought within.

For if Somnolencia succumbed to the Rise of Passive Laziness, then all would truly be lost.

21

The Rise of Passive Laziness

At first, no one noticed.

In the wake of The Fall of Busyness, life in Somnolencia had never been better.

The former workers of Perpetuopolis had embraced the art of relaxation, replacing their strict schedules with morning naps, mid-afternoon naps, and post-dinner pre-sleep dozing.

The Nap Academies were flourishing, with new students eager to learn the secrets of deep, undisturbed slumber.

The Pillow Prophecies were recited at grand gatherings, reminding the citizens that "True peace lies in stillness."

And yet, something was amiss.

Zzzocrates noticed it first.

There was a difference between resting and simply never moving again.

It began with small things:

The Council of Naps stopped holding meetings, because getting up was too much effort.

Messages were left unread, because reading required focus.

Even yawning was sometimes skipped because it was too strenuous.

Then, entire projects of leisure were abandoned.

The Great Pillow Fortress, a monument of comfort, was left unfinished because the builders decided even stacking cushions was exhausting.

The Nap Tournaments, once a fierce competition of the most skilled snoozers, were cancelled because contestants couldn't be bothered to show up.

And worst of all -

The Great Nap Festival, the most sacred event in all of Somnolencia, was delayed indefinitely.

Because no one could summon the energy to organize it.

It was the golden age of laziness, but something had gone terribly wrong.

Zzzocrates watched in horror as the once peaceful and balanced world of Somnolencia tipped into complete and utter stagnation.

Not because of tyranny.

Not because of oppression.

But because, no one cared enough to do anything anymore.

The Whispered Warning

Deep within the Hall of Perpetual Rest, where the oldest and wisest snoozers lay in an eternal state of half-slumber, a warning began to circulate.

An old prophecy, long forgotten, hidden within the final pages of the Pillow Prophecies:

"Beware the day when stillness turns to stagnation.

When dreams are dreamt but never pursued.

When the art of leisure becomes the curse of inaction.

For when all wakefulness is abandoned."

"The Dreaming will consume all."

Zzzocrates felt a deep, uneasy chill settle over him.

Had they fought so hard against Sir Industrious, only to fall into a different kind of trap?

Had the fight for rest led them to a world where nothing ever happened again?

He could not allow it.

Somnolencia had thrived on balance - on the beauty of rest, but also on the joy of waking up just long enough to appreciate it.

But how could he convince a nation of unmoving dreamers that some things were still worth doing?

There was only one solution.

A debate.

A grand, legendary, never-before-attempted Laziness Debate.

Where the wisest minds of Somnolencia would gather, argue, and perhaps, find a way to reclaim the true essence of leisure.

If he could rouse them from their state of absolute idleness, he might just save Somnolencia from itself.

And so, the word was sent out slowly, and with minimal effort, of course.

The Great Laziness Debate was about to begin.

22

The Great Laziness Debate

For the first time in ages, the Council of Naps convened.

Well… sort of.

Some attended virtually through dream projection (since physically moving was too much effort).

Others sent pre-recorded yawns as their official statements.

A few were physically carried in their beds, so they wouldn't have to wake up completely.

But despite these minor challenges, the debate was happening.

The sleepiest philosophers, wisest procrastinators, and legendary snooze sages had gathered at the Hall of Comfortable Inaction to answer one simple, but crucial question:

Had Somnolencia become too lazy for its own good?

The Argument for Ultimate Rest

On one side, Snorri the Still, the grandmaster of Passive Laziness, argued passionately (or, at least, as passionately as one could while reclining).

"We have fought hard for our right to do nothing!" he declared.

"Why should we abandon the perfect stillness we have achieved? This is the golden age of rest - an era where no one is forced to move, think, or even acknowledge time itself!"

He waved a weighted blanket over his head, a symbol of the ultimate comfort they had won.

"We have defeated Busyness. We have cast out Industriousness. We have built a world where time means nothing, schedules are myths, and even the most ambitious dream eventually dissolves into the grand, eternal nap."

The crowd murmured in agreement, though some were too tired to complete a full murmur and just nodded very, very slowly.

Had they not earned the right to pure, uninterrupted idleness?

The Case for Balanced Laziness

But then, Zzzocrates stood or rather, slightly adjusted his recline to be at a more authoritative angle.

"Yes, we have defeated the tyranny of busyness," he began.

"But let me ask you all, when was the last time you even bothered to change sleeping positions?"

A ripple of mild discomfort spread through the room.

For some, it had been days.

For others, weeks.

And then came his most daring argument.

"Tell me, my fellow dreamers, have we stopped living altogether?"

A hush fell over the assembled snoozers.

Had they gone too far? Had leisure turned to lifelessness?

Even Snorri the Still furrowed his drowsy brow.

The Proposal: The Grand Awakening (But Not Really)

Zzzocrates, sensing the shifting tides, laid out his vision.

"What if, instead of absolute inaction, we practiced selective effort?"

Gasps.

Snorri clutched his blanket.

Others stirred for the first time in ages.

"I propose a simple change," Zzzocrates continued.

"One moment a day, we do something, just to remind ourselves we're alive."

Snorri scoffed.

"And what would this 'something' be?"

"It can be anything!" Zzzocrates countered.

"A leisurely stretch. A well-timed sigh. Even an elegant turn to the cooler side of the pillow. Nothing excessive, of course - we are not beasts!"

Murmurs of interest rippled through the crowd.

Could this be the next evolution of laziness?

A world where rest was still sacred, but one or two small motions a day were considered acceptable?

It was unthinkable, but also oddly appealing.

After several hours of deliberation (and an unscheduled nap break), the vote was cast.

By an overwhelmingly sluggish majority, it was decided:

Somnolencia would embrace Selective Effort.

A single, tiny action per day.

A monumental shift in philosophy.

Zzzocrates smiled as he reclined further into his chair.

"This is the dawn of a new era.".

23

Busyness is Not the Same as Productivity

The Great Mistake of the Wakeful World

Deep in the heart of Somnolencia, within the Library of Forgotten Tasks, the Nap Scholars unearthed a shocking revelation.

The Wakeful World misunderstood productivity entirely.

They equated being busy with being useful.

They filled their days with endless meetings, deadlines, and urgent-but-meaningless tasks, yet,

Nothing of real value ever seemed to get done.

Sir Industrious, before his glorious downfall, had been their most tragic example.

He had worked tirelessly, but toward what? A world that never slept. A people who never rested.

Fools.

The Wakeful World had lost sight of what truly mattered. And now, it was time to prove them wrong.

The Doctrine of Efficient Idleness

The Council of Naps, now emboldened by their victory in the Great Laziness Debate, sought to redefine work itself.

Zzzocrates, fresh from his philosophical triumph, presented a new argument:

"True productivity is not about how much you do. It is about how little you need to do to achieve the best result."

Gasps.

Murmurs of enlightenment.

Even Snorri the Still blinked once - a rare sign of extreme excitement.

Could it be that the Wakeful World's obsession with activity was actually making them less effective?

It was time to test this theory.

The Great Laziness Experiment

A challenge was issued to the Wakeful World.

A group of diligent, workaholic overachievers would compete against a team of Somnolencian sleep enthusiasts.

The goal? Complete a complex problem in the most effective way possible.

The Wakeful World champions arrived armed with planners, schedules, coffee, and an unhealthy dose of urgency.

The Somnolencians arrived in pajamas, carrying pillows, sipping chamomile tea.

The Wakeful Ones immediately sprang into action, racing against time.

Meanwhile, the Somnolencians, napped.

Hours passed. The Wakeful Ones toiled, argued, and revised their work repeatedly.

The Somnolencians occasionally woke up to offer a single, insightful thought, then dozed off again.

By the end of the day, the results were clear:

The Wakeful Ones had produced hundreds of pages of frantic work, filled with errors, unnecessary complexity, and contradictions.

The Somnolencians had produced one beautifully simple, efficient solution, because they had rested, thought clearly, and only acted when absolutely necessary.

The world was stunned.

Was it possible that doing less, actually meant achieving more?

The whispers began to spread.

The Wakeful Ones started doubting their methods.

Could Somnolencia's do-nothing philosophy be the answer to their endless struggles?

Zzzocrates simply smiled, stretched, and rolled onto his other side.

"Efficiency," he mused, "is the art of knowing when to stop."

The Great Demonstration

After the Great Laziness Experiment shook the foundations of the Wakeful World, whispers of a new kind of wisdom began to spread.

But the sceptics were still many.

They still believed that constant effort was the only way forward.

And so, to settle the matter once and for all, the Council of Naps announced The Great Demonstration - a final test that would prove, beyond doubt, that rest was not a hindrance but a necessity.

This time, the entire Wakeful World would bear witness.

The Contest of Effort vs Ease

The stage was set in the Plaza of Perpetual Motion, where the Wakeful Ones gathered, eager to watch the Somnolencians fail.

On one side stood Team Industrious - composed of the brightest, most overworked minds of the Wakeful World.

Armed with alarm clocks, energy drinks, and an unhealthy fear of wasted time, they were determined to show that hard work always triumphed over laziness.

On the other side lay Team Somnolencia - draped in blankets, sipping herbal tea, and yawning confidently.

Their only tools? patience, clarity, and naps.

The challenge?

A series of increasingly difficult tasks - from solving a major logistical problem to writing a powerful speech, all the way to devising a sustainable way of life for the future.

The only rule?

Each team could work however they pleased.

The Contest Begins

At the sound of the First Bell, Team Industrious launched into a frenzy of movement.

They brainstormed, debated, scribbled notes, erased them, rewrote them, debated some more, until their table was buried under papers, stress, and the unmistakable scent of burnout.

Meanwhile, Team Somnolencia, closed their eyes.

Gasps of horror rippled through the crowd.

"They're wasting time!" the Wakeful Ones whispered.

But the Snooze Sages knew better.

They allowed their dreams to settle, their thoughts to align, their minds to drift toward clarity.

Every once in a while, one of them would wake up, murmur an insight, and roll over.

Slowly but surely, their solutions came together, effortless, elegant, and perfectly clear.

Hours passed. The Final Bell tolled.

The results were examined.

Team Industrious had produced dozens of unfinished ideas, conflicting solutions, and a nervous breakdown or two.

Team Somnolencia had produced a single, flawless strategy, refined in their dreams and spoken in just a few sentences.

A hush fell over the crowd.

Then,

A slow realization dawned.

The greatest solutions did not come from frantic effort,

They came from a rested mind.

The Awakening of the Wakeful Ones

One by one, the Wakeful Ones began to lower their alarm clocks.

The Perpetual Motion Enthusiasts rubbed their eyes, suddenly aware of how tired they were.

Even Sir Industrious' former followers exchanged nervous glances, their confidence shaken.

Had they truly been wrong all along?

The answer came from a most unexpected place.

The very same elders of the Wakeful World, those who had spent their lives pushing for endless productivity, now stared in awe at Team Somnolencia.

One of them, an ancient CEO of busyness, stepped forward.

With trembling hands, he removed his golden wristwatch, a symbol of time's relentless rule.

And in a voice heavy with realization, he uttered the words that would change the world forever:

"Perhaps… it is time to rest."

<u>The Necessity of Rest</u>

With the Great Demonstration concluded, the world stood at a crossroads.

The Wakeful Ones, long convinced that unceasing effort was the only way to success, now found themselves staring into the abyss of their own exhaustion.

Cities of constant movement had turned into ruins of burnout.

Workers who had never taken a break now found themselves unable to perform even the simplest of tasks.

Leaders, who once glorified the hustle, now whispered in secret about how their minds had grown foggy, unstable, and dangerously inefficient.

And in the midst of all this, a single question echoed across the land:

"Have we been pushing too hard for too long?"

The Council of Naps Issues Its Final Warning

In Somnolencia, the Council of Naps gathered for a final decree.

This was no longer a debate.

This was a crisis.

If the world did not rest soon, something far worse than simple exhaustion would take hold.

A condition spoken of only in hushed whispers.

A fate so dire that even the most stubborn wakeful minds feared it.

They called it The Hollowing - the moment when one loses the ability to rest entirely.

Once the mind forgets how to sleep, it does not simply keep going,

It breaks.

It was happening already.

And unless something was done, it would soon spread across every corner of the world.

The Call for a Universal Rest Period

At sunrise, the Herald of Yawns - Somnolencia's most skilled messenger, stood atop the Tower of Tranquility and sent forth the decree.

For the first time in recorded history, the world would pause.

A universal rest period would be enforced.

The Great Factories of Busyness would be silenced.

The Treadmills of Relentless Motion would be stopped.

The Stock Exchange of Never-Ending Deals would be put to sleep.

For one full month, the world would rest.

Nations would embrace slowness.

People would rediscover the art of doing nothing.

And at the end of it, perhaps, just perhaps, humanity would remember what it meant to truly live.

The Sleepless One Watches from Afar

But not everyone welcomed this new era.

In the shadows of Perpetuopolis, where the remnants of Sir Industrious' followers still clung to the old ways, a figure stood unmoving.

A legend.

A nightmare.

A man whose eyes had never once closed - who had transcended exhaustion itself.

He had watched the fall of Sir Industrious.

He had seen the Council of Naps reclaim their power.

And now, as the world prepared to embrace rest, he made his move.

He had many names, but history would remember him as Sir Never-Stops - The Sleepless One.

And he had only one goal:

To eradicate the very concept of rest, once and for all.

24

The Arrival of the Sleepless One, Sir Never-Stops

Long before the fall of Sir Industrious, there were rumours.

Whispers of one who had conquered sleep entirely - a figure so consumed by productivity that even exhaustion dared not touch him.

But these were just myths, weren't they?

A cautionary tale to frighten overworked apprentices in the offices of Perpetuopolis?

A story told to insomniacs who refused to rest, warning them of what lay at the end of endless wakefulness?

But now, he was here.

Sir Never-Stops, The Sleepless One.

His eyes, deep and sunken, burned with an unnatural energy.

His skin, pallid and untouched by the warmth of rest, seemed to vibrate ever so slightly, as if his very being had forgotten stillness.

And his presence carried an eerie hum - a sound not of breathing, not of heartbeat, but of a relentless force that never ceased, never wavered, never paused.

The world had seen wakefulness, but never like this.

For Sir Never-Stops had not merely rejected sleep - he had transcended it.

And he had come to finish what Sir Industrious had started.

The Sleepless Crusade Begins

With Perpetuopolis still smoldering from the collapse of its Great Engine, the remaining Wakeful Ones gathered around their new leader.

"Sleep," he said, his voice cold and precise, "is a disease."

A weakness that held humanity back.

And he would cure the world of it.

Where Sir Industrious had sought to conquer laziness, Sir Never-Stops sought something far greater, the complete eradication of rest itself.

No naps.

No pauses.

No moments of stillness.

A world of pure, uninterrupted action.

His followers, already conditioned by decades of anti-rest propaganda, cheered in exhausted agreement.

And so, the Crusade of the Sleepless began.

While the world of Somnolencia prepared for its Universal Rest Period, the Sleepless Ones plotted their invasion.

They would strike when the world was at its most vulnerable.

And by the time anyone realized what had happened, it would be too late.

The Dream of the Tireless One Calls

But deep within the ruins of Perpetuopolis, something stirred.

In the abandoned Hall of Relentless Effort, where Sir Industrious had once proclaimed his vision of ceaseless productivity, a whisper echoed through the dust.

A voice.

A presence.

Some believed that Sir Industrious had been defeated.

Some believed he had fallen into an eternal slumber, finally overcome by the exhaustion he had refused to acknowledge.

But they were wrong.

For Sir Industrious was not gone.

He was waiting.

And as Sir Never-Stops prepared his crusade, the world would soon learn a terrible truth,

The Tireless One still dreamed.

And in that dream, he was still working.

25

The Dream of the Tireless One, Sir Industrious

For most, sleep is a retreat - a surrender to the gentle arms of rest.

But for Sir Industrious, it was a prison.

After his fall, the great champion of ceaseless work had been cast into the realm of forced slumber - a punishment most would consider a mercy.

Yet even in the deepest chambers of unconsciousness, Sir Industrious did not rest.

No, he laboured.

Within his dream, he built factories of thought, constructed endless assembly lines of ideas, and forged an empire of motion that churned without pause.

The world of Somnolencia had put him to sleep, but they had forgotten one crucial thing -

Even a dream can be weaponized.

The Nightmare of Productivity

Deep within the landscape of his unconscious mind, Sir Industrious had built the impossible:

A realm of pure efficiency, untouched by the sluggishness of flesh, free from the limitations of exhaustion.

A place where one could work forever without the burden of fatigue.

He called it The Eternal Assembly - a vast, otherworldly production floor where machines hummed, gears turned, and labour was endless.

But it was not just a dream.

Slowly, his thoughts began to seep into reality.

His old followers, those who had not surrendered to Somnolencia's rule, began to hear his voice in their restless nights.

They saw his vision.

They felt his unceasing will.

And they answered.

Across the lands, in dark corners where sleep had grown uneasy, the remnants of Sir Industrious' loyalists began to stir.

The time for action was approaching.

But Sir Industrious could not return alone.

He needed something more.

He needed an army.

He needed a Council.

And so, as his influence bled into the waking world, a new power began to rise -

The Council of Endless Motion.

26

The Council of Endless Motion

The echoes of Sir Industrious' dream had spread far and wide, infiltrating the minds of those who had once sworn loyalty to his vision. In the darkened corners of Somnolencia, where torches burned long into the night, murmurs of rebellion grew louder. The Sleepwalkers, those who had once danced on the edge of both worlds, began to stir with uncertainty. The Yawn Knights, protectors of restful slumber, felt the first ripples of disturbance in the Dreamscape.

And in the farthest reaches of Perpetuopolis, where rest had been outlawed and the clock never ceased to tick, the faithful still toiled. These were the Sleepless Engineers, the Timekeepers, the Watchers of the Unyielding Hours. They had waited for a sign, and now, their leader's dream had called them back to the cause.

At the heart of Perpetuopolis, hidden beneath the ruins of abandoned timekeeping towers, the Council of Endless Motion assembled for the first time since the Great Nap War.

They came from different factions, each with their own philosophy of perpetual activity:

Lady Multitaska – The Mistress of Simultaneity, who could write reports, attend meetings, and file grievances against inefficiency all at once. Her mind never settled, and she considered sleep an outdated relic of a less-evolved species.

Master Urgency – The Master of Deadlines, who spoke only in the language of pressing matters and whose presence alone caused anxiety to rise in those around him.

The Mechanized Overseer – A being rumoured to be neither fully man nor fully machine, constructed from the remnants of broken alarm clocks and discarded schedules.

The Taskmasters' Triad – A trio of bureaucratic enforcers who ensured that productivity quotas were met, even if it meant breaking the very fabric of time itself.

As they gathered in their hidden chamber, the air was thick with tension. A single, rhythmic ticking sound echoed through the chamber - a metronome set to the pace of endless industry.

Lady Multitaska was the first to speak. "We have been dormant for too long. Sleep has ruled this land uncontested, but the time of inefficiency must come to an end."

Master Urgency leaned forward, his voice clipped and precise. "Every moment wasted is a betrayal to the cause. Sir Industrious has sent us his vision. He still dreams of a world where no second is lost to idleness."

The Mechanized Overseer's gears whirred as it processed the discussion. "The productivity initiative must be revived. The Great Engine of Perpetual Motion must turn once more."

They all turned to the grand hourglass that stood in the center of the chamber. Its sands had been frozen since the day Sir Industrious fell. Now, the first grains of sand trickled downward, a sign that the slumbering giant was beginning to wake.

The council had only one purpose: to prepare the world for the return of their leader.

The Call to Arms

Throughout Somnolencia, strange disturbances began to unfold. Sleep grew uneasy. Rest was interrupted by whispers of urgency. The sacred fields of Dreamgrass, where the most tranquil naps were taken, began to wither.

Yawnrick, the Grand Dozer of Somnolencia, was the first to notice the change. His once-constant drowsiness was fading, replaced by an unfamiliar alertness. He summoned the Council of Naps, but even among the most devoted sleepers, worry had set in.

"This is unnatural," murmured Snorelina, the High Priestess of the Nap Temples. "Something stirs in the deep hours of the night. A force unseen, but felt."

The Nap Scholars turned their eyes to the stars, where the patterns of sleep and wakefulness had remained undisturbed for centuries. Now, the constellations of Rest and Repose flickered, as though something powerful sought to erase them.

And in the farthest reaches of the Dreamscape, the Nocturnal Scribes found ancient warnings within The Pillow Prophecies, scriptures written by sages long past.

"The Waker will rise,

When dreams are seized,

And the storm of Wakefulness

Shall break the night."

The Awakening Storm Approaches

The Council of Endless Motion had begun their work. Productivity Cultists infiltrated towns, sowing seeds of unrest. The Dreamwatchers reported sightings of strange, shadowy figures moving in the corners of the night, disrupting sleep with whispers of urgency.

And deep within the dream-prison where Sir Industrious lay, something shifted. His fingers twitched. His breath grew steady. The dream-world around him pulsed with energy.

The storm was coming.

27

The Awakening Storm

The skies over Somnolencia had never been more troubled. Where once the gentle hues of twilight reigned, now a chaotic swirl of shifting shadows and silver streaks coursed through the heavens. The winds whispered of unease, rustling the leaves of the great Slumbering Willows, disturbing the tranquil rhythm of a realm that had long basked in the philosophy of rest.

The Council of Endless Motion had risen, their influence creeping into the dreams of the weary, sowing seeds of unrest. At first, it had been subtle, an occasional thought of unfinished work, an inexplicable urge to move when one should be still. Then, the waking hours grew longer, the desire to rest diminished, and with it, the harmony of Somnolencia began to wane.

Yawnrick, the Grand Keeper of the Snooze Sceptre, felt the change deep within his bones. Standing atop the Observatory of Stillness, he watched as the distant edges of Somnolencia flickered lights that should have dimmed in sleep now burned with unnatural persistence. The storm was not just a force of nature; it was a herald of conflict. A war between philosophies, between those who wished to embrace slumber and those who sought to banish it forever.

And at the heart of it all was Sir Industrious, whispering from the void of his forced slumber, orchestrating the movements of his devoted followers from within his endless dream.

The Unrest Grows

The first true signs of battle were not fought with swords but with willpower. The Council of Endless Motion had found its way into the thoughts of Somnolencia's people, and the effects were undeniable. The once-serene streets of Napshire and Dozeington grew tense with an unfamiliar energy. Productivity Meetings, a concept unheard of in Somnolencia began cropping up in secret. Sleepwalkers, once the guardians of balance, now found themselves torn between their duty to Somnolencia and the inexplicable desire to march toward the growing storm.

Lady Multitaska, the newly revealed strategist of the Council, led the charge. Unlike the raw, relentless power of Sir Industrious, she was a different kind of menace. Her words were smooth, persuasive. She did not demand obedience, she simply presented choices, and in doing so, made the very act of stillness feel like negligence.

"You could nap," she would say, her voice slithering through restless minds, "or you could accomplish something."

Some resisted, but others faltered, and as the days passed, the world teetered closer to a breaking point.

The Tempest Breaks

Then came the storm. Not of wind and rain, but of sheer, unrelenting force. The borders of Somnolencia trembled as the Council of Endless Motion made their first true move – a shockwave of pure wakefulness surged through the land, an unnatural energy rippling across the once-peaceful land.

The great Slumbering Willows, ancient trees that had stood for eons as symbols of tranquillity, began to shake violently. Some, unable to withstand the force of motion, cracked and fell, their deep-rooted connection to the Dreamscape severed.

The Sleeper's Bell, a relic used only in times of dire emergency, was rung, its deep chime reverberating through the land. The people of Somnolencia stirred, realizing that the age of peace had officially ended.

Yawnrick gathered the Council of Naps. The time for passive resistance was over. They would have to stand, not merely as defenders of sleep, but as warriors of stillness.

"The Battle of the Sleepwalker approaches," he declared, his voice steady despite the chaos surrounding him. "We must prepare for the greatest challenge Somnolencia has ever faced."

28

The Battle of the Sleepwalker

In the heart of Somnolencia, beneath the pale glow of the Twin Moons of Drowsia, an eerie procession moved through the city's slumbering streets. They were neither fully asleep nor fully awake, an army caught between two worlds, trapped in the ethereal haze of half-consciousness. These were the Sleepwalkers, the last line of defence against the coming storm.

Among them stood Yawnrick the Drowsy, the reluctant leader of the resistance, wrapped in the Cloak of Coma. His eyelids fluttered, half-shut as always, yet his mind teetered at the precipice of total stillness and forced vigilance. To his right, Lady Dozella whispered, "The time has come, Yawnrick. The Council of Endless Motion grows stronger. We must meet them at the Veil of Dreams."

Yawnrick sighed - a slow, drawn-out exhale that sent ripples through the dream-realm. He did not want a battle. No true Somnolencian did. But the Sleepwalkers had been called, and so they marched.

The March to the Dreamveil

The Veil of Dreams was the last barrier between Somnolencia and the influence of Sir Industrious. It was a place where waking and sleeping overlapped, where thoughts could shape reality. The Sleepwalkers arrived just as the first signs of unrest began to manifest strange distortions in the dreamscape, mechanical chimes ringing out where silence once reigned, the scent of burning oil creeping into the air.

From the shadows beyond the Veil, the Council of Endless Motion emerged.

Lady Multitaska stood at the forefront, her eyes darting between a dozen phantom ledgers, her hands scribbling calculations in the air. Behind her, the Chronomancers weaved the Chains of Urgency, attempting to bind time itself to their will. And towering above them all, the spectral vision of Sir Industrious loomed, still trapped within his dream but exerting his influence upon the waking world.

A battle unlike any other was about to begin.

The Clash of Sleep and Wakefulness

The first wave of the Council's forces struck swiftly. The Chronomancers unleashed a barrage of Deadline Spears, each one infused with a sense of impending doom. The Sleepwalkers staggered; their dreamlike pace unable to keep up with the sudden rush of imposed urgency. Some collapsed, jolted into full wakefulness, vanishing into the waking world, lost to the cause.

But Yawnrick held his ground.

With a deep, reverberating yawn, he countered with the Echo of Fatigue—a wave of irresistible drowsiness that washed over the battlefield. The Chronomancers faltered, their calculations slowing, their hands growing heavier. Lady Multitaska stumbled, momentarily overwhelmed by the sheer stillness of it all.

The battle raged on. Sleepwalkers drifted through the mist like ghosts, evading attacks with movements too sluggish to be anticipated. The Council countered with bursts of Coffee Mist, attempting to jolt them back into full wakefulness. Reality itself began to crack under the strain of the opposing forces, as the Veil of Dreams twisted and frayed.

Then, from the rift above, came the first whispers of something greater.

The Call of the Dreamers

As the battle reached its peak, the dreamscape itself began to shift. Beyond the battlefield, beyond the conflict, something ancient stirred. Deep within the Forgotten Slumber, where only the most devoted to rest had ever ventured, the Dreamers - Somnolencia's oldest sages began to awaken.

They had long slept, watching over the realm in silence. But now, their time had come.

And as the first Dreamer opened their eyes, the battle was about to change forever.

29

The Awakening of the Dreamers

For centuries, the Dreamers of Somnolencia had been the guardians of the deepest realms of slumber, keepers of a sacred, undisturbed rest. Their existence was one of harmony, floating effortlessly in a state of perpetual dozing, their collective dreams weaving the fabric of Somnolencia's tranquillity.

But now, their peace was under siege.

The war between sleep and wakefulness had reached their sacred domain, and the echoes of conflict rippled through the very fabric of dreams. Sir Industrious and his Council of Endless Motion had not only fractured the balance of rest but had begun pulling the unwilling from their slumber, forcing them into wakefulness against their will.

The Dreamers felt it.

A slow, creeping force pulling at their minds, whispering of obligations, responsibilities, and the horrors of unfinished tasks.

For the first time in eons, they stirred.

And the moment they did, they realized the terrible truth - if they did not rise now, there would be no sleep left to return to.

The Call of the Sleepless Ones

The Dreamveil, a vast plane of floating islands where the Dreamers resided, had begun to shake. Once a realm of peace, it now quivered with unease, the tendrils of Sir Industrious' unrelenting will seeping through.

Yawnrick, still weary from the Siege of Slumberville, stood before the Council of Napkeepers, who had long served as advisors to the Dreamers.

"The balance is crumbling," Yawnrick pleaded. "Sir Industrious has found a way to twist even dreams into his weapons. If the Dreamers do not awaken now, they may never wake again."

The Napkeepers - robed figures of vast wisdom and slumberous knowledge, sighed in unison, their collective exhale carrying the weight of endless rest.

"The Dreamers are not meant to awaken," one of them intoned. "They are the guardians of deep slumber, not warriors of wakefulness."

"But if they do not awaken," Yawnrick countered, "then Somnolencia will fall. And once the land is consumed by motion, even dreams will be shackled to purpose."

A deep silence followed.

The Dreamers themselves, hovering in their sleep-bound state, murmured within their dreams. Some had already begun to shift uneasily, sensing the disturbances.

And then, the first Dreamer opened an eye.

It was a slow, languid motion, but it carried the weight of eternity.

Then another followed.

And another.

Soon, hundreds of Dreamers, who had long remained in an endless state of blissful sleep, were awakening.

And with them, their power returned.

The Power of the Dreamers

The moment the Dreamers stirred, the air in Somnolencia shifted.

Where once the forces of wakefulness had begun creeping into every corner, a counterforce now emerged.

Dream-energy, ancient and boundless, began to weave its way back into the land. The fog of urgency and forced motion that Sir Industrious had spread began to waver.

From their resting places, the Dreamers descended, their presence a calming wave over the battlefield of sleep and wakefulness.

But with their awakening, a terrible truth was revealed,

The Dreamveil itself, the very foundation of Somnolencia's deepest rest, had begun to crack.

It was no longer enough to resist.

No longer enough to stall the forces of wakefulness.

They had to fight.

They had to reclaim sleep.

And so, the Dreamers, ancient and once removed from worldly affairs, prepared for battle.

The War of Waking and Sleeping had begun.

30

The War of Waking and Sleeping

The skies over Somnolencia darkened, not with storm clouds, but with something far more ominous - the rising tension between sleep and ceaseless motion.

Sir Industrious and his Council of Endless Motion had rallied their forces, a vast army of the wakeful, their eyes wide with restless energy. The caffeine-fuelled zealots, the sleepless scribes, the tireless workers - each driven by a singular purpose: to eradicate slumber once and for all.

Their banners, stitched with gears and ticking clocks, fluttered over their marching legions. Their battle cries were not shouts, but the relentless tapping of keyboards, the clanking of tools, the unending hum of production.

And at their heart, The Engine of Perpetual Motion.

A massive, towering construct of whirring gears and glowing dials, the Engine was Sir Industrious' greatest creation. It fed on wakefulness, pulling in the restless energy of the sleepless and converting it into an ever-growing force of productivity. It was the antithesis of Somnolencia itself.

If it was not stopped, sleep would no longer exist.

The Dreamers, now fully awakened, stood on the other side of the battlefield, their once-tranquil expressions hardened with purpose. Yawnrick, the reluctant hero, found himself at the front lines, alongside the Council of Napkeepers and the Sleepwalkers, their movements slow but resolute.

"For too long, we have allowed urgency to dictate our fate!" Yawnrick declared, his voice carrying across the land. "Tonight, we remind the world that rest is not weakness, that slumber is not surrender. We fight for dreams! We fight for sleep!"

And with that, the war began.

The Clash of Ideals

The battlefield was unlike any in history.

On one side, the Sleepless charged forward, their feet never pausing, their hands moving with restless efficiency. They wielded alarm clocks as weapons, firing sonic bursts of urgency. Bureaucrats on rolling office chairs zipped through the ranks, issuing summons to wakefulness.

On the other side, the Sleepwalkers met them in kind, moving as one, their drowsy steps weaving through attacks with effortless grace. The Napkeepers chanted the ancient lullabies, their melodies wrapping around their enemies, pulling them into unexpected moments of drowsiness.

And the Dreamers, they reshaped the battlefield itself.

With every step, they conjured visions of peace, weaving illusions of soft beds and endless fields of slumber. They turned the sky into a swirling cosmos of drowsy comfort, and the air grew thick with the scent of lavender and warm blankets.

But Sir Industrious was prepared.

He stood atop the Engine of Perpetual Motion, his eyes burning with sleepless intensity.

"You think your dreams will stop us?" he bellowed. "You think you can lull us into submission? WE DO NOT YIELD! WE DO NOT SLEEP! WE"

His words were cut short as Yawnrick hurled a Sacred Pillow of the Ancients at him, knocking him clean off his perch.

The battlefield erupted in chaos.

The Machine Must Fall

Despite the Dreamers' best efforts, the Engine of Perpetual Motion remained untouched, humming with an eerie, ever-growing power.

It was the heart of Sir Industrious' army.

And as long as it ran, they could not truly win.

The Dreamers knew what had to be done.

They had to break the machine.

But to do that, they would have to reach it first.

And so, the final phase of the battle began.

The Dreamers, the Napkeepers, and the last defenders of slumber launched a desperate assault toward the towering construct. Sir Industrious, now back on his feet, summoned his last, most terrifying forces - the Enforcers of Urgency, the Clockwork Sentinels, and the Caffeinated Berserkers.

The fate of Somnolencia now hung in the balance.

And as Yawnrick and his allies made their final push toward the Engine, the great assault began.

The Breaking of the Engine.

31

The Breaking of the Engine and the Assault on the Engine

The battlefield trembled under the weight of two opposing forces, the defenders of slumber and the relentless engines of wakefulness.

At the heart of it all stood the Engine of Perpetual Motion, a monstrous, grinding machine that spewed out urgency, fuelling the sleepless army with endless energy. It ticked and whirred with a nightmarish rhythm, pulsing like a heart that refused to stop beating.

Sir Industrious, battered but unyielding, stood atop the great metal beast, his voice a whip of command.

"You will never stop this machine! You may break your pillows against it, drown it in your lullabies, but it will keep turning! As long as there is work to be done, we will never rest!"

His words sent waves of renewed Vigor through his followers. The Caffeinated Berserkers howled, their hands twitching with jittery energy. The Clockwork Sentinels whirred to life, their gears spinning in synchronized motion. The Bureaucrats of Endless Toil pulled out fresh stacks of paperwork, drowning their enemies in unread memos.

It was an unrelenting storm of wakefulness.

But the Dreamers had one thing the sleepless did not.

The ability to surrender.

Not to work. Not to urgency. But to peace.

And so, they launched their final assault.

The First Breach

Yawnrick led the charge, flanked by the greatest warriors of Somnolencia - the Sleepwalkers, gliding forward like ghosts; the Napkeepers, whispering lullabies that curled through the air like spells; and the Masters of the Snooze, carrying the Sacred Blanket of Absolute Comfort.

Their goal was clear:

They had to stop the Engine.

But the machine was more than metal and gears. It was an idea, an ideology forged into steel.

To break it, they had to shatter the illusion that work could never end.

And so, the Sleepwalkers did something radical.

Instead of fighting, they let go.

One by one, they collapsed to the ground - not in exhaustion, but in perfect, deliberate surrender. They did not resist; they did not fight. They simply rested.

And in doing so, they created a ripple in the battle itself.

The Bureaucrats of Endless Toil hesitated.

The Caffeinated Berserkers blinked, their limbs slowing, their movements suddenly unsteady.

The illusion of unending energy began to crack.

The Engine Begins to Falter

Sir Industrious roared from atop the machine, desperately turning dials and pulling levers.

"No! The work is not finished! We do not stop! We NEVER STOP!"

But the Engine began to stutter.

It had always relied on the belief that stopping was impossible. That motion was inevitable.

But now, sleep was spreading like a quiet revolution.

The Dreamers pressed forward. The Napkeepers unfurled the Sacred Blanket of Absolute Comfort, draping it over the Engine's core. The warm, velvety fabric smothered the machine's relentless ticking, muffling the sound of urgency itself.

The gears shuddered. The hum of motion turned into a groan.

For the first time since its creation, the Engine of Perpetual Motion hesitated.

Sir Industrious screamed in fury.

But it was too late.

With a final push, Yawnrick hurled The Pillow of Infinite Reprieve into the heart of the Engine.

The machine let out a sigh,

and stopped.

The Fall of Perpetual Wakefulness

Silence swept over the battlefield.

The moment the Engine ceased, its influence collapsed.

The Bureaucrats of Endless Toil dropped their pens, suddenly realizing they had no desire to fill out another report.

The Caffeinated Berserkers, their energy drained, sank to the ground in confusion.

Even the Clockwork Sentinels ground to a halt, their mechanisms no longer powered by the relentless drive of wakefulness.

For the first time in ages, Somnolencia was free from urgency.

But as the dust settled, something else became clear,

This was not just the fall of a machine.

It was the fall of a city.

The great metropolis that Sir Industrious had built - the towering, sleepless hub of endless work began to crumble.

Without the Engine, Perpetuopolis, the City of Endless Motion, could not sustain itself.

The buildings, powered by ceaseless energy, began to power down.

The great factories slowed, their gears stiffening.

The streets, once packed with moving bodies, fell into a strange and unfamiliar stillness.

And then, with a final, inevitable sigh - Perpetuopolis began to collapse.

32

The Collapse of Perpetuopolis

Perpetuopolis had once been a marvel of industry - a place where clocks never stopped ticking, where workers never stopped moving, where the very idea of idleness had been stamped out like an unforgivable crime.

It had been built by the sleepless, for the sleepless.

Its towers stretched toward the sky, not out of ambition, but necessity - higher and higher, layer upon layer, just to fit more offices, more schedules, more quotas.

Its streets had been rivers of relentless movement, flowing with tired yet obedient souls marching from one task to the next.

And at its center had stood the Engine of Perpetual Motion, the throbbing heart that had kept it all running.

But now, that heart had stopped.

And without it, Perpetuopolis was dying.

The Crumbling Towers of Industry

The change began slowly, so subtle that no one noticed at first.

A few flickering streetlights.

A handful of executives who, for the first time in their lives, found themselves sitting down and wondering, "What now?"

Then, entire conveyor belts shuddered to a halt, leaving assembly lines of unfinished products - millions of identical productivity planners, left forever blank.

And then, finally, the buildings began to crack.

The skyscrapers of Endless Ambition, the towers of Unceasing Progress - they had not been designed to withstand stillness. Their walls had only ever been reinforced by the sheer momentum of constant activity.

And without that motion, they could not stand.

One by one, the great symbols of wakefulness began to collapse.

The Department of Nonstop Planning crumbled under its own weight, burying its final, uncompleted five-year strategy.

The Arena of Eternal Meetings fell silent for the first time since its construction.

The Skyscraper of Productivity, where workers had climbed higher and higher without pause, finally stopped mid-task, its uppermost floors left forever unfinished.

The City That Never Slept was finally closing its eyes.

Sir Never-Stops and Sir Industrious: A Last Stand Against Stillness

Amidst the chaos, two figures refused to accept reality.

Sir Industrious, kneeling in the rubble, stared at the wreckage of his life's work.

"This isn't real. It cannot be real," he whispered, his hands shaking as he tried to reignite a dead console. "It can still be fixed. It must be fixed."

But the gears would not turn.

The numbers refused to rise.

For the first time in his existence, there was nothing left to do.

And then there was Sir Never-Stops.

Unlike Sir Industrious, who had ruled through planning and efficiency, Sir Never-Stops had thrived purely on raw, untamed motion. He had been the embodiment of hustle - running from meeting to meeting, never slowing down, never pausing for thought.

And now, as the city fell, he did the only thing he had ever known how to do -

He ran.

Through the collapsing streets, past the burning wreckage of schedules and task lists, he kept moving.

If he could just keep going, just outrun the stillness, then maybe, just maybe, he could survive.

But stillness was everywhere.

Like a creeping force, it wrapped around the city, dulling its once-electric pulse.

And no matter how fast he ran - it was catching up to him.

For the first time, Sir Never-Stops felt a terrible, crushing weight pulling at him.

Fatigue.

It was foreign to him. Alien. Unacceptable.

But as his legs slowed, as his breath came in sharp gasps, he finally understood.

There was no more running.

There was no more motion.

There was only rest.

And then - for the first time in his existence, Sir Never-Stops… stopped.

The Last Glance at a Dying City

From the outskirts of Perpetuopolis, Yawnrick and the Dreamers watched as the last great towers fell, as the sleepless kingdom dissolved into history.

The war was not over.

Sir Industrious still lived.

And so long as he lived, there was always a chance that wakefulness would rise again.

But for now, the Dreamers had won a great victory.

As the dust settled, a deep hush fell over the city, not the silence of defeat, but the silence of peace.

And somewhere, in the very depths of Perpetuopolis, Sir Industrious sat among the ruins, staring into the quiet.

For the first time in his life, he had no plan.

And that terrified him more than anything else.

33

The Fall of Sir Never-Stops and Sir Industrious

Sir Never-Stops had spent his entire existence in motion.

Running from place to place, from meeting to meeting, from crisis to crisis.

He had believed that if he never paused, never allowed himself even a moment of stillness, then rest could never catch him.

But now, in the ruins of Perpetuopolis, there was nothing left to run to.

His once-powerful strides had turned sluggish. His breath came in shallow gasps. His mind, which had once been razor-sharp with urgency, now felt slow, hazy - too quiet.

The world around him blurred.

The city that had thrived on motion was now eerily silent.

And worst of all, his own body had betrayed him.

His legs refused to move.

His head tilted forward.

His eyelids - heavy, leaden began to close.

A great terror seized him.

Was this… surrender?

No. No, it could not be. He would fight it. He would,

But his body did not listen.

For the first time, Sir Never-Stops did something unthinkable.

He collapsed.

Face-first, onto the cold ground of his fallen empire.

And there, where he had once ruled over perpetual motion, he finally, truly, completely - stopped.

And the moment he did, sleep - the great enemy he had spent his life avoiding, finally took him.

The Tyranny of the Empty Mind

But Sir Industrious did not collapse.

He did not fall.

Instead, he sat - amidst the ruins of his great work, hands folded, gaze fixed on nothing.

Still.

Motionless.

But not in rest.

No, there was no rest for him.

His mind, unchained from the world of action, had turned inward - an infinite, inescapable loop of thought, a relentless storm of plans and calculations.

With every breath, he rebuilt Perpetuopolis in his head.

He saw the towers rise once more.

He felt the gears of the Engine of Perpetual Motion turning again.

He imagined the schedules being restored, the meetings reconvened, the great march of progress resuming.

But it was only in his mind.

In reality, there was nothing left.

And that - that was the true horror.

For all his life, Sir Industrious had believed in work. Not work for joy, not work for fulfilment, but work for the sake of work itself.

And now, for the first time, he had nothing to do.

No quotas to meet.

No systems to optimize.

No great task left to complete.

And that emptiness, that unbearable void, was his true defeat.

He clutched at his own temples, trying to force his mind into action.

There had to be something left.

There had to be work still undone.

But there wasn't.

And in that moment, Sir Industrious - the great architect of motion, became truly lost.

Lost, not in rest, but in the terrifying realization that he had no purpose beyond motion.

For the first time, he understood why Somnolencia had won.

Not through battle.

Not through sabotage.

But because they had something he could never understand - peace.

And he, who had spent his life fighting against stillness, had nothing left but the unbearable weight of his own mind.

A mind that could not stop.

But now, had nowhere left to go.

A World Without Its Champions

Perpetuopolis had fallen.

Sir Never-Stops had succumbed to sleep.

Sir Industrious had succumbed to thought.

And across the world, the last remnants of the Wakeful Order dissolved into stillness.

For the first time in a long, long while,

Somnolencia was at peace.

But peace is not the end of a story.

No, the Dreamers knew this truth well.

Because while they had won a great battle, another storm was brewing.

Something was stirring beneath the surface of sleep itself.

And soon, they would learn:

Even victory can be disrupted by an awakening.

34

The Sleepwalkers Stir

The ruins of Perpetuopolis lay silent. After the collapse of Sir Industrious' great empire, its once-buzzing streets were now filled with nothing but a sluggish wind that carried echoes of unfinished tasks. The Great Awakening had been thwarted, and Somnolencia rejoiced in the restoration of its sacred leisure.

But deep within the Dreamscape, something had changed.

The Pillow Prophecies spoke of many things - of sacred naps, of legendary blankets, and of The Dozing Sage, but one passage had long been ignored, dismissed as nothing more than an old bedtime tale:

Beware the Sleepwalkers, for they dwell in the limbo between wake and rest. Neither truly asleep nor fully awake, they drift endlessly, lost in the tides of dreams they can never leave.

Few had given it thought. Until now.

In the days following the fall of Perpetuopolis, strange disturbances began rippling through the slumbering world. At first, it was small things, dreams flickering like faulty candlelight, yawns that never fully escaped lips, the unsettling sensation of movement during deep sleep.

Then, the reports came.

"Something walks through dreams," whispered the nap sages.

"I awoke standing at my doorstep, though I never left my bed," muttered a concerned citizen.

"There are figures in the fog," murmured another. "Drifting, staring but never blinking."

Yawnrick the Restful called an emergency meeting of the Council of Naps. The Napfluencers were summoned, along with Professor Slumberson Hustlebane and Lady Multitaska. Even Zzzocrates, who had been deep in meditation upon The Golden Blanket of Eternal Rest, stirred from his contemplation.

"These disturbances cannot be ignored," Yawnrick declared, rubbing his temples. "Whatever lurks in the Dreamscape is stirring. And I fear it is connected to the collapse of Sir Industrious."

Professor Slumberson adjusted his spectacles. "There is a theory, A dangerous one. When Industrious and Never-Stops pushed their followers beyond exhaustion, they shattered the balance. Some souls, unable to remain awake yet unwilling to surrender to rest, may have crossed into another state. A state neither here nor there."

"Sleepwalkers," whispered Lady Multitaska, her voice unusually solemn.

The word sent a ripple of unease through the chamber.

"Then we must stop them," said the Napfluencers. "Surely, if they cannot wake nor sleep, we must help them find their way back."

Zzzocrates, ever wise, shook his head. "You do not understand. The Sleepwalkers have no way back. They are echoes of those who tried to defy the rhythm of rest. And now, they drift, searching."

"Searching for what?" someone asked hesitantly.

A silence fell. Then, a whisper, carried by the Dreamscape itself, slithered into their ears:

For purpose. For something to fill the void where sleep once dwelled.

And deep within the shadows of Perpetuopolis, a group of Sleepless survivors - the last remnants of Sir Industrious' devoted followers, watched the drifting figures with awe.

"They are neither awake nor asleep," one of them murmured. "They are… perfect."

The leader of the Sleepless, a gaunt-eyed figure with a manic grin, stepped forward. "No," he said, his voice trembling with excitement. "They are the future."

And with that, the first steps toward a new, more terrifying movement began.

35

The Return of the Sleepwalkers

At first, the Sleepwalkers were nothing more than a strange curiosity.

Somnolencians, used to the occasional case of nighttime wandering, assumed it was merely an odd phase - perhaps a side effect of too much evening tea.

But then it spread.

What began as a few isolated incidents soon turned into an epidemic of unnatural movement.

Throughout Somnolencia, more and more people rose in the middle of the night, their eyes vacant, their steps slow but relentless.

They did not speak.

They did not respond.

They simply walked.

And they did not stop.

By the third night, the streets were filled with silent processions of those caught in the grip of something neither sleep nor wakefulness.

And that was when the Dream Weavers confirmed their worst fear.

The Sleepwalkers had truly returned.

The Half-Waking Curse

Unlike Sir Industrious' followers, who had fought to stay awake, and unlike the true citizens of Somnolencia, who embraced rest, the Sleepwalkers were trapped.

Neither here nor there.

Neither asleep nor awake.

Caught in a state of perpetual, mindless motion, their bodies obeyed commands that had not been given, moving without purpose, without destination.

And the worst part?

It was spreading.

Those who got too close to a Sleepwalker found themselves drawn into their trance.

A single brush of contact.

A moment of exposure.

And soon, they too would rise in the night, staring blankly ahead, joining the march of the restless.

The Nap Scholars called it The Half-Waking Curse.

And if it wasn't stopped, Somnolencia itself would be overrun.

Not by productivity.

Not by industry.

But by a sleep so broken that it would never end.

A Desperate Search for Answers

The Council of Naps convened an emergency session.

Yawnrick, now wearing The Weighted Blanket of Authority, called upon the wisest dreamers, the laziest sages, and the fluffiest pillow-makers for counsel.

The Pillow Prophecies were consulted.

The Archives of Forgotten Naps were searched.

And finally, the answer was found.

The Sleepwalkers had last been seen during the First Age of Wakefulness.

Long before the rise of Somnolencia, when the world was torn between work and exhaustion, the Sleepwalkers had been the first to fall.

They were the ones who had tried to do both - who had refused to rest but also could not truly stay awake.

Their bodies had adapted to neither state.

They had wandered endlessly until the ancient Dream Weavers, in a desperate act, sealed them into the deepest layers of sleep, ensuring they would never rise again.

But something had broken the seal.

Something had let them out.

And now, Somnolencia had to find a way to stop them, before they spread beyond control.

The Stirring of the Sleepless

But not everyone feared the return of the Sleepwalkers.

In the ruins of Perpetuopolis, something else was stirring.

Far beneath the city, in the abandoned halls of motion, a meeting was taking place.

A meeting of those who had once served Sir Industrious and Sir Never-Stops.

The remnants of the Wakeful Order.

The last survivors of the Productivity Empire.

They watched as Somnolencia panicked.

They watched as the Sleepwalkers filled the streets.

And slowly, a realization dawned upon them.

This was their moment.

The downfall of Perpetuopolis had broken them.

But now, Somnolencia was vulnerable.

Its people distracted.

Its defenders scrambling for answers.

And if ever there was a time to strike,

It was now.

The Sleepless were not finished.

They would rise again.

They would take back what was lost.

And this time, there would be no rest.

36

The Last Stand of the Sleepless

For years, the Sleepless had whispered in the dark corners of Perpetuopolis, clinging to the embers of their broken empire.

They had watched as Sir Industrious fell.

They had witnessed the collapse of the Eternal Assembly.

And yet, they refused to surrender.

Now, as the Sleepwalkers marched through Somnolencia, lost in their endless trance, the Sleepless saw their chance.

If the world would not wake willingly, then they would force it.

The Siege of Somnolencia

Under the command of Marshal Ever-Vigil, the last of the Sleepless legions marched forth.

Though their numbers were small, their minds burned with relentless will.

No exhaustion.

No hesitation.

No doubt.

Their weapons were forged from pure wakefulness, alarms that never stopped ringing, coffee that burned hotter than fire, and gears that turned without end.

And they had one goal:

To tear Somnolencia from its slumber and shatter the dream forever.

With the Sleepwalkers spreading chaos, the defenders of Somnolencia were stretched thin.

The Nap Guard, led by Yawnrick, struggled to contain the rising tide of the Half-Waking Curse.

The Dream Weavers were scattered, working desperately to reseal the breach.

And deep beneath the Grand Pillow Citadel, the Dreamveil - the last barrier between Somnolencia and endless waking - began to crack.

If the Sleepless reached it, if they shattered the final wall between sleep and wakefulness -

Somnolencia would be lost.

The War of Rest and Restlessness

The battle that followed was unlike any before.

The Sleepless stormed the dreamlike streets, wielding blinding beams of fluorescent office lighting, weapons of endless productivity reports, and chains of never-ending deadlines.

They forced the citizens awake, breaking through layers of peace and relaxation.

The Nap Guard, weary but determined, countered with shields of softness, lullabies of ancient power, and weighted blankets that could subdue even the most restless soul.

Yawnrick himself stood at the gates of the Dreamveil, facing down Marshal Ever-Vigil.

"You fight for a world without rest," Yawnrick said, voice heavy but resolute.

"I fight for a world without waste," Ever-Vigil countered. "A world where nothing is lost to sleep. Where every moment is used."

"But what is life without rest?" Yawnrick asked. "Without dreams?"

Ever-Vigil hesitated.

And in that moment, Yawnrick struck - hurling a Pillow of Absolute Comfort directly at the Marshal.

The impact was immediate.

For the first time in years, Ever-Vigil felt softness.

His body, conditioned for endless motion, faltered.

His mind, trained for ceaseless calculation, slowed.

His eyes, which had never closed in sleep, began to droop.

And then, for the first time in his life, he yawned.

It was over.

One by one, the Sleepless fell.

Not to violence.

Not to force.

But to the unstoppable power of rest.

Some fought it.

Some resisted.

But the truth was undeniable.

They were tired.

And as the lullabies of the Dream Weavers filled the sky, the Sleepless finally succumbed to the one thing they feared most.

Sleep.

A Fractured Dreamveil

But the battle had come at a cost.

Though the Sleepless had been defeated, the strain on the Dreamveil was immense.

The clash of waking and sleeping had pushed the barrier to its limits.

And as the last of the Sleepless drifted into unconsciousness, a terrible sound echoed across Somnolencia.

A deep, rumbling crack.

The Dreamveil was breaking.

And beyond it, something stirred.

Something old.

Something forgotten.

Something that should never have been awakened.

The final battle had been won.

But the greatest danger was yet to come.

37

The Fall of the Sleepless and the Shattering of the Dreamveil

Silence fell over Somnolencia.

The war had ended.

The once-mighty forces of the Sleepless lay scattered across the dreamlike fields, their weapons of perpetual wakefulness discarded, their restless energy drained.

No alarms rang.

No schedules loomed.

Only the soft sound of steady, peaceful breathing filled the air.

Even Sir Never-Stops, the last true disciple of sleeplessness, had surrendered to the one force he had fought all his life:

Rest.

But peace had come at a price.

The Dreamveil - the ancient barrier that had kept the waking world and the dream world in balance, had cracked beyond repair.

And as it crumbled, something long hidden began to stir.

A force older than waking. Older than sleep itself.

The Dreamveil Breaks

At the heart of Somnolencia, where dreams were woven and the fabric of rest was stitched, the Dreamveil shattered.

The sky split open with a luminous, swirling mist - a chasm between two realities.

For the first time in history, dreams and wakefulness existed side by side.

All across the world, people experienced something new:

The hyper-efficient office worker, once enslaved to the ticking of the clock, suddenly felt the weight of time ease.

The overburdened student, lost in endless exams, saw their mind slow, their thoughts clear.

The factory labourer, worn down by the grind of existence, paused - for the first time, they truly paused.

Somnolencia had not just saved itself.

It had changed the world.

But this new reality was fragile. If left unchecked, the balance between waking and sleeping could spiral into chaos.

Something had to be done.

And so, the Dream Weavers and the last remnants of the Nap Guard gathered at the ruins of the Dreamveil to do the unthinkable.

They would not rebuild it.

They would reinvent it.

The Invention of Somnolencia: The Great Nap Conductor

From the remains of the Dreamveil, an invention was forged - The Great Nap Conductor.

A device neither of waking nor of dreaming, but a harmony of both.

Neither a wall nor a cage, but a rhythm - a natural pulse that flowed between work and rest, action and inaction, wakefulness and slumber.

This device would not force sleep upon the world, nor would it banish wakefulness.

Instead, it would guide people back to balance.

With a single chime, it could slow the restless mind.

With a single wave, it could remind the weary that rest is not weakness.

It was the final gift of Somnolencia to the world.

And with it, the age of endless exhaustion came to an end.

As the citizens of Somnolencia gathered to witness the first activation of the Great Nap Conductor, Yawnrick stepped forward.

He had fought long and hard for this moment.

And now, he would speak to the world beyond Somnolencia.

His voice echoed through the realms, reaching not just the land of sleep, but the cities of wakefulness, the restless corners of the earth where people had forgotten how to pause.

"You were told that to stop is to fall behind.

That to rest is to fail.

That exhaustion is the price of success."

"But that was a lie."

"Rest is not the enemy. Sleep is not a curse. In the quiet of stillness, in the depth of dreams, we do not lose ourselves - we find ourselves."

"So, to all who hear this, wherever you are, remember:

The world does not crumble when you pause.

The world does not end when you rest.

Let go. Breathe. Sleep.

And wake up, truly awake."

As his words faded, the Great Nap Conductor hummed for the first time - a gentle, calming resonance that swept across

Somnolencia, through the lands of waking, and into the hearts of all who had forgotten the power of rest.

It was the beginning of a new era.

An era where wakefulness and slumber were no longer enemies.

An era where laziness was no longer a curse, but a form of wisdom.

The Nap That Conquered the World

The battle had ended. The engines had collapsed, the sleepless citadels had crumbled, and the last cries of resistance had faded into the hush of slumber. Somnolencia stood victorious, not through brute force or relentless struggle, but through the quiet, undeniable power of rest.

As the golden rays of a dream-lit dawn stretched across the sky, a hush settled over the world. For the first time in an age, peace was not measured in productivity, but in the depth of a sigh, in the weight of a head finding its pillow without fear.

Perpetuopolis, the city of unyielding wakefulness, was no more. Its citizens, once bound by the chains of endless motion, lay upon the ruins of their own ambition - resting, breathing, dreaming. Their eyes, once filled with exhaustion and defiance, fluttered closed as the first true sleep in generations overtook them.

The Sleepless Age had ended.

A Message to the World

To those who chase time as if it can be caught - pause.

To those who measure life by toil alone - breathe.

To those who believe that movement is the only sign of progress - close your eyes and listen.

For too long, the world has been enslaved by the myth of endless motion. We have worshipped busyness as virtue, built towering monuments to work, and mistaken exhaustion for achievement. We have convinced ourselves that success is measured in sweat, that purpose is defined by productivity, and that stopping, even for a moment is a sign of weakness.

But what if we have been looking at it all wrong?

What if true innovation does not emerge from relentless striving but from the quiet spaces in between? What if history's greatest ideas were not forged in the fires of urgency but in the stillness of contemplation? What if the key to a better world is not doing more, but being more?

Somnolencia has always known the secret the world refuses to see: Rest is not the enemy of progress. It is its foundation. A mind that never slows down cannot dream. A heart that never pauses cannot feel. A soul that never rests cannot create.

We were not born to be machines, endlessly toiling, endlessly optimizing, endlessly sacrificing joy for the illusion of efficiency. We were born to wonder, to wander, to sleep beneath the sky and wake with new dreams. To let our thoughts drift like clouds, unhurried, unburdened, free.

And so, to those who have forgotten: Remember.

Pause.

Breathe.

Dream.

For it is in dreams that the world is truly changed.

The Unfinished Dream

As the people of Somnolencia drifted into a well-earned slumber, their dreams filled with the serenity of victory, the world beyond did not sleep so easily. In the distant horizon, past the lands where rest reigned supreme, an ember of unrest smouldered.

Not all had embraced the stillness.

In the forgotten corners of time, where schedules once ruled and ambition never yielded, something stirred. A hum, faint yet deliberate, vibrated through the silence - a promise, a warning.

Rest had won the battle.

But the war between stillness and ceaseless motion was far from over.